REDEMPTION

THE STORY OF JONAH

REDEMPTION

A HISTORICAL NOVEL

SUSAN DAYLEY

To Mark—my best friend, my husband, and my home.

Also, to the children of my school classes, who got to know about Jonah with me in ways we didn't expect.

Walnut Springs Press, LLC
110 South 800 West
Brigham City, Utah 84302
http://walnutspringspress.blogspot.com

ISBN: 978-1-935217-50-3

ACKNOWLEDGEMENTS

First of all, I am grateful to my husband, Mark, who is always enthusiastic about my writing. When I'd read him passages of this story, he'd interrupt me just to gush, "That is so good." (I wish I could imbue his enthusiasm into all my readers!) His feedback and ideas about *The Terrible City* were invaluable, as were his frequent offers to take care of household duties so I would be free to write. I'd also like to thank Mark for turning my rough idea of an old typewriter into a functioning, cool website.

I'd like to thank my mother for her encouragement and her willingness to read the story in its various phases. And I appreciate everyone who has been excited for me during this journey.

Many thanks to Michael Morris, whose expertise, help, and encouragement gave me hope.

Finally, thank you to my editor, Linda Prince, for her patience, professionalism, and skill. I appreciated that she saw in my manuscript a story worth sharing.

Map 1

Kingdoms at the time of Jonah

Damascus

KINGDOM OF
DAMASCUS

Sidon

Zeraphath

PHOENICIA

Tyre

Acco

Sea of Chinnereth

Mt.
Carmel

Gath-
hepher

Jazreel Valley

Ramoth-gilead

SCALE OF MILES

0   10   20   30   40

Dor

Dothan

River Jordan

Samaria

Israel

The
Great
Sea

Joppa

Bethel

JERUSALEM

AMMON

Gaza

PHILISTIA

Lake Asphaltitis
(Dead Sea)

Judah

MOAB

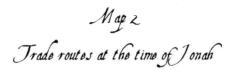

Map 2

Trade routes at the time of Jonah

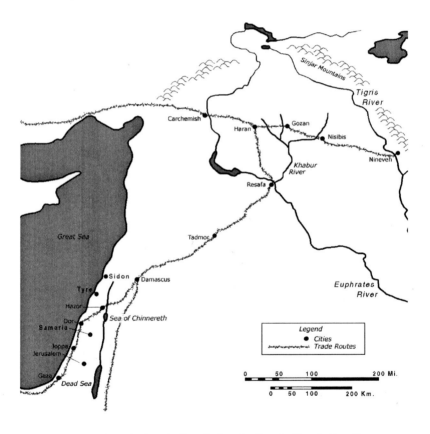

Sinjar Mountains

Tigris River

Carchemish

Haran

Gozan

Nisibis

Nineveh

Khabur River

Resafa

Tadmor

Great Sea

Sidon

Damascus

Tyre

Hazor

Dor

Sea of Chinnereth

Samaria

Joppa

Jerusalem

Gaza

Dead Sea

Euphrates River

Legend

● Cities

Trade Routes

0   50   100   200 Mi.

0   50   100   200 Km.

This is the rejoicing city that dwelt carelessly, that said in her heart, I am, and there is none beside me.

Zephaniah 2:15

Prologue

∽∾∽∾∽∾∽∾∽∾∽∾∽∾∽∾

ong, long ago—nearly 800 years before Jesus Christ was born into mortality, 230 years before Daniel was cast into a den of lions (554 BC), about 150 years before Aesop was born (620 BC), and approximately 30 years before Romulus laid the foundation of the city of Rome (753 BC), lived a reluctant prophet and thrived a magnificent city that was mightier than the mightiest. In about 785 BC, the choices of those living in that city would surprise many, including that same prophet.

In the middle of a vast, green world flourished the great and terrible civilization known as the Assyrian Empire. Through the middle of this most terrible of empires ran two legendary rivers: the Euphrates and the Tigris. These two rivers stretched from the mountains above the land of Mesopotamia to where they joined beyond the great city of Ur, hundreds of miles away. From there the waters continued onward to divide into many small outlets, sink into salt marshes, and finally drain into the Gulf of Persia.

The Euphrates and the Tigris were the main highways for trade among the cities of Assyria and the lands beyond. Sooner or later, from the caravans to the west bringing goods from the Great Sea, or rafts traveling up the Tigris River with wares from the populous cities to the south, all that man had to trade arrived at the center of commerce and power. This city, built larger by stages through a succession of kings, would soon become the capital of the Assyrian Empire—the beautiful, vast, and wicked city of Nineveh. Nineveh lay on the eastern bank of the Tigris, across the river from the modern-day city of Mosul, Iraq. Nineveh was built on a plain, and through the middle of the city flowed the Khawsar River, which joined the Tigris.

Nineveh stretched along the banks of the Tigris River for about seven and a half miles. From the river, the city stretched east toward the hills. Yet the province of Nineveh was even larger. The Old Testament states, "Nineveh was an exceeding great city of three days' journey" (Jonah 3:3). The city grew to include the communities of Nimroud, Kouyunjik, Khorsabad, and Karamless. Each of these four royal estates, built in succession by kings or rulers of Assyria, contained palaces, statues, gardens, and tree-filled parks surrounded by walls as if they were individual cities. During the reign of Sennacherib, walls were built to encompass the city, joining the four estates. These walls were forty to one hundred feet high and broad enough for three chariots to drive side by side along the top. High towers rose from the walls of Nineveh, which featured no less than fifteen main gates into the city.

The palaces of Nineveh were lined with calcite alabaster slabs brought from the quarries of Egypt and carved into pictures of conquests, brutalities, captured slaves, and pagan gods. Massive carved figures also featured winged females wearing garlands or carrying a fir cone or other religious emblem. Ivory and gold leaf ornamented chairs, tablets, walls, and pillars. Carved to emerge from the alabaster walls were winged sphinxes, lions, bulls, kings, soldiers, slaves, lotus flowers, and scrolls.

At Kouyunjik, winged, human-headed bulls from fourteen to sixteen feet square formed the entrance. The carvings at Khorsabad were not as large as the ones at Kouyunjik, but they featured more detail. In the center palace of Nimroud was a hall with four entrances formed by colossal, human-headed lions and bulls. These colossi stood through the ages of men, looking blindly away from their doings, their passionless faces disregarding those who had created them.

Between the palaces of Nineveh, families lived in tents or simple houses made from mud bricks. These houses were neat, with tables, couches, chairs, and—always—separate apartments for the women. Many Assyrian houses enclosed prized gardens and orchards. Throughout the city, water from the Tigris River, from the foothills of the Kurdish Mountains to the north, and from the Khawsar River was directed into canals to irrigate the farms, gardens, and orchards. From tent poles hung vases filled with clear water so that it might cool in the shade of tent shadows. There were also many cattle pastures within the city.

Together, these enclosed palaces, fountains, and parks—and among them, the smaller houses, huts, tents, gardens, farms, and pastures—formed the great city of Nineveh.

Everything in Nineveh moved to the pace of a growing empire. There were slaves to tend cattle and serve in the palaces. There were sculptors and artists constantly at work within the palaces or carving in cuneiform on large stone tablets for the city's library. (One day it would be the greatest library in the world, with more than 22,000 clay tablets. It would contain the accounts of the conquests of Assyria, the story of the Great Flood, the epic of Gilgamesh, and other books on history, law, and religion.)

There were gardens to tend, fruit to pick, children to rear, produce to take to market, baskets to fill, and dinners to prepare. There were soldiers and guards in constant drill, and horses to exercise, groom, and feed. There were camels to unload of the goods they brought, and boats to empty. And the motion behind it all—even in the still of the night when the men and women of Nineveh rested, when nothing could be heard but the occasional bellow of a camel or the cry of a child—was the constant flow of the Tigris.

Beyond the beauty of Nineveh, though, was an enduring darkness, because Nineveh was a city enriched by the spoils of war that had come home with its returning soldiers. "In the palace at Kouyunjik, engraved in bas-relief into an alabaster slab was represented the invasion of a mountainous country. The enemy defended the summit of a wooded hill against Assyrian warriors, who were scaling the rocks, supporting themselves with their spears and with poles, or drawing themselves up by the branches of trees. Others, returning from the combat, were descending the mountains, driving captives before them, or carrying away the heads of the slain" (Austen Henry Layard, *Nineveh and Its Remains* [London: John Murray, Albermarle Street, 1850]; spelling standardized).

It was just one of countless battles recorded on the palace walls. Such scenes always displayed the brutality of wanton conquest and merciless treatment of conquered people. And darker still, beyond the wicked, bloodthirsty quest for power and the indolent life of plundered riches and slaves, was the daily worshipping of pagan gods with sexual sins and human sacrifice. For along with the fabrics, ornaments, and household goods that came to Nineveh, there came also storytellers, philosophers, false gods, and abominations of foreign lands. In Assyria, dark ideas accumulated; in Nineveh they flourished.

The time had come for God to send a prophet to this city.

And it came to pass after a while, that the brook dried up,
because there had been no rain in the land. And the word of
the Lord came unto him [Elijah], saying, Arise, get thee to
Zarephath, which belongeth to Zidon, and dwell there: behold,
I have commanded a widow woman there to sustain thee.

1 Kings 17:7–9

Chapter One

∽∾∽∾∽∾∽∾∽∾∽∾∽∾∽

The young widow gazed into the barrel, knowing its contents would be the same meager grains she had left there the night before. She gripped the rim and slowly lowered the large earthen jar onto the floor, propping it against the rug she had rolled up to stabilize it with. By kneeling on the floor, she could reach her right arm into the barrel up to her shoulder. There, with a knife and her fingers, she began to scoop the remaining meal into a wooden bowl.

The knock at the door startled her. "Mother, there is a visitor," her young son called out. Afraid he would answer it, exposing her in an awkward position, she dropped her tools, stood up, and immediately set the barrel upright again, the bowl and knife now inside.

"Jonah, please sit on your stool," she whispered as she adjusted her shawl to cover her head.

Her pale, hungry son meekly obeyed. The knock came again, but she had moved across the room and was able to open the door even as the man's hand was lifting for a third tap.

The widow did not recognize the man, and she immediately thought of the law regarding the giving of hospitality to strangers. Despair crossed her face, for she knew there would not be enough meal. But the man spoke before she could invite him in.

"Go to the city gate to gather sticks for a fire. There the Lord's servant will find thee." Then he turned and walked away.

For a moment she watched his retreating form disappear into the shadows of the approaching twilight. However, three minutes later she had reassured her son and carefully closed the door of her home behind her. She did not know which bewildered her more, the surprise command by the messenger, or that she had left her son to go do as the stranger had directed. She passed the pottery workshops and kilns of Zarephath. The industry of the town had slowed little during the famine; they still traded their jars with Sidon and Tyre, which were major seaports of the Phoenicians. But the trade that provided beautiful objects and clothes did not bring food when there was none to be had. The drought was severe and stretched far.

She left the city by the narrow, southern gate where the road to Tyre stretched. She had not asked which gate she was to go to, but had simply gone to the one closest to her home, being too weak herself to consider doing otherwise. Outside the gate, she obediently began to search for sticks beneath the dying trees of the drought-filled land. The ground had already been gleaned of dry twigs, and most of the lower branches of the trees had been broken off. Then she saw two sticks that had blown down during the night that had not yet been claimed. She stooped to pick them up, reflecting that she was not in need of a big fire for so small a meal.

She raised her head when she heard the footsteps along the road, and there she saw a man with a long, gray beard, wrapped in the rags of what had once been fine robes. She waited as he drew nearer. "Fetch me," he called out hoarsely, "I pray thee, a little water in a vessel that I may drink."

Clearly, this old man was worn from his journey. The young mother gently helped him to sit in the shade beneath a tree that still clung to a few shriveled leaves. Then, scooping to pick up the two meager sticks she had set down, she assured him, "There is still water in the well of the town. I will hasten there and return quickly." She gathered up her skirts with her right hand so that her feet would be unencumbered by them. She was concerned that she was away from her son too long, and hurried toward the city gate as quickly as her own feeble strength would allow.

She stopped short when she heard the old man call after her again. Turning around slowly she heard him ask what she had feared.

"Bring me, I pray thee, a morsel of bread in thine hand."

His voice pierced her heart, but she knew she could not refuse. She had been commanded to come by the messenger, who said this man was the servant of the Lord, but she would have obeyed regardless; the tradition of hospitality was too strong. Still, it was so much to ask! In weak protest she explained, "I have not a cake, but only a handful of meal in a barrel, and a little oil in a cruse." Then to emphasize her plight she held out the sticks in her left hand and added, "Behold I am gathering two sticks that I may go in and dress it for me and my son that we may eat it, and die."

Her pitiful words hung in the dry, windless day, then seemed to drift away into eternity. Then the man said, "Fear not; go and do as thou hast said; but first make me a little cake of the meal, and bring it unto me, and after make for thee and for thy son."

She opened her mouth to protest again, but then she closed it and turned with her head bowed to do as he bid. What did it matter? But the raspy voice called to her again, and though there was now more distance between her and the old man beneath the tree, she heard each word clearly. She turned to stare at him even as he spoke.

"For thus saith the Lord God of Israel" —the voice was surprisingly strong— "the barrel of meal shall not waste, neither shall the cruse of oil fail, until the day that the Lord sendeth rain upon the earth."

She gasped as she stood there, and the words repeated themselves in her mind. Then the leaves above her rustled in a breeze and several broke free to fall around her like a soft, brown rain. Suddenly her heart rejoiced. "I will return."

Back in her small home, she again tipped the barrel and dug out the meal. She mixed it with some water and the drops of oil from a clay bottle, making a cake the size of her palm. Then she built a tiny fire with the two sticks and baked the small cake in a flat pan on the fire. Her son watched her silently, but when she wrapped the cake in a cloth, picked up their now-empty water vessel, and reached to open the door, he spoke, "Mother, where do you take our cake? Will there be no supper for us?"

"Jonah, there will be supper for us, but you must wait a bit longer. I am taking this cake to a man who serves the Lord."

"Where is this man?"

"He is outside the city gate. I will not be long." Then she was gone and hurrying to where she had left the older man.

She paused at the city well and lowered the bucket. She felt it reach the bottom and tip on its side to receive some of the shallow water at the bottom. When she pulled up the bucket, it was only partially filled with brownish water. But it was as she had expected, and she poured it into the vessel she had brought from home. Then she hurried again toward the gate.

The old man was walking to meet her. His rest had apparently done him good, but the water she gave him and the small cake fortified him with a forgotten strength. He smiled and insisted on carrying the water vessel for her.

At the door to her home she paused, then awkwardly tried to explain, "I am a widow—my husband is dead, but you are welcome to stay with my son and me."

"Thank you," he replied simply and opened the door for her to pass through.

After the old man had sat down, there was an awkward moment as she realized she had promised her son she would return to make him a meal. Then Elijah spoke, "Do not be afraid to look in the barrel. The Lord has promised there would be enough. You demonstrated your faith by serving his prophet, putting the will of the Lord before your own concerns. Go and prepare the cakes for you and your son."

Slowly the widow walked to the large earthen jar. She did not look inside as she positioned the rug and again lowered it by the rim to the floor. Somehow it seemed a bit more stable as if the bottom had been weighted. Then, as she knelt to scoop meal into her bowl, she looked into the shadowy depths and realized the knife would be inadequate. The bottom was covered with rich golden meal that was now spilling toward her. She gasped a great sob back and withdrew to get a cup.

"Mother!" Jonah called with concern. "Why are you crying?"

"Come see, Jonah," his mother held out her hand for him,

tears streaming down her face. "Come see the miracle the Lord has provided."

Suddenly the mother could no longer contain her sobs of joy and wonder. She ran to the privacy of the other room, where much of their food had been kept before the famine. Now it was where she slept, surrounded by empty jars and a pile of sacks. She went to her knees beside a chest that sat untouched in the corner. "O, Lord of heaven, thou hast looked down upon this small house and blessed it by sending thy servant to us. And in this time of want, thou hast blessed us that we are provided for. I thank thee for the meal that does not waste and the oil that does not fail." Her voice caught. It was a miracle that would be told through the centuries of mankind, but to her, in her own small world, it was a miracle that spoke of how the Lord loved and cared for her and her son. "I cannot give back to thee, who art the Master of all, but I offer my life to thee. I will serve thy servant as long as I am needed. And my son" —she paused as she thought of her son, her only child and comfort— "and my son I will have taught that he may grow up to serve thee." She whispered the words, making a covenant to give her son to the Lord. A deep peace settled on her and she stayed by her bed a while longer.

When she tipped the cruse the oil did not drip, but poured in a thin, steady stream. Later, as she and her son were eating their cakes (the old man, who was sitting on a bench near the window, spoke, "My name is Elijah. I am the Lord's prophet. While I stay with you it will be as the Lord has promised and you will have food to eat. Tomorrow, we will talk to the men of the town about digging the well deeper. The Spirit of the Lord has told me that there is more water, but we must dig."

The woman looked up, tears still on her cheeks, and a smile

lighting her face. "After much sorrow," she said, "it is good to have hope."

There was a pause as the old man looked deeply into her eyes as if examining her soul. Then he probed gently, "Tell me of your sorrow."

The young widow sighed, then pushed back her chair and carried her dish and her son's dish to be washed in a basin of warm water over the small fire. There, with her head bent over her task, she began to speak. "My husband, Amittai of Gath-hepher, died when our son was but five. I returned to Zarephath to be near my mother and so that my father could train my son in the word of God. Last year when the famine was first severe, my mother died, and this spring my father died. Now there is no family for me but Jonah." She indicated the lad who sat across from her at the table.

"How old is your son?" Elijah asked.

"He is now eight."

"And who teaches him?"

"There is no one," the young woman said with a sigh.

"Then while the famine lasts, I will stay and I will teach the lad," Elijah declared. "The Lord has a work planned for your son."

The woman had no response, but suddenly she found herself laughing and rejoicing. "The Lord has heard my prayers," she said, reaching out to hug her son.

It was the beginning of hopeful, happy days in the small house near the southern gate of Zarephath. Elijah, who had gained much strength, was given a place to sleep in a loft above the now-empty goat shed behind the house. The young housewife watched the prophet mount the ladder easily, as if he were not as ancient as his wrinkled face and hands suggested.

Each day he took his meals with the widow and her son, and

after breakfast he would read with the son from the scrolls the widow had kept from her father's house. Elijah taught Jonah his prayers, and told him the stories of Abraham, Isaac, Jacob, King David, and many others.

The prophet met with the men of the city, and each of the town's wells was dug deeper, starting with the one near the widow's house. People often came to visit with Elijah and ask for his blessings. They were grateful to have plenty of fresh water, but even more so to have the Lord's prophet with them, giving them living water—the word of God.

And each day the widow would go to the barrel and find more than enough meal in the bottom to fashion cakes for the day. It was a cold, scarce winter, but the little home always had food to eat and stories by the small fire. Each day Elijah would go out and return with an armful of sticks. The widow was never certain where he managed to find the wood when supplies were becoming rarer. The well near their home kept providing water, and each day Jonah learned more. So even in the scarcity, there was plenty to be grateful for.

Then one morning, after Elijah had been there five moons, the young mother arose early, her heart filling with happiness to see the sunlight streaming in the eastern window of her home. It was a warm, friendly light that seemed to seek out every dusty corner. Spring had arrived. Grabbing a broom, she swept the floor with a vigor she hadn't felt in a long time. Next. she went to the well and filled a bucket with water, and then began to scrub every inch of her small home with its two rooms and the lean-to addition where her son slept.

That day she fetched extra water to launder all the clothes and blankets in the house. As she was collecting bedding from the room she slept in, she stood facing the old chest she had avoided since her husband died. Taking a deep breath, she laid the bedding down and crossed the room to kneel beside the chest. The young mother gripped the sides and lifted the lid that was unsecured, revealing the contents she had put off sorting through. Then, she began to carefully remove them one by one, using her apron to wipe the dust from each and set it aside. There in the bottom, beneath her husband's keepsakes of shells, a prayer shawl, and several scrolls, was a beautiful glass vase from Sidon. She removed it gently, sure it was to have been a gift for her. The anniversary of her birth was a week after he had died. She stroked the vase tenderly, then set it on her bed. The scrolls she set aside for Jonah's studies. Finally, in the bottom of the chest, she touched a robe that had once been her husband's. It was still sturdy, and later that day she laundered it and gave it to Elijah.

"Thank you," he said sincerely.

"It is to thank you!"

She was glad to see that he seemed to stand a bit taller now that his rags were tossed away. She filled the vase with early spring flowers and sat it on the table.

Within a week, however, tragedy came to the cheerful little household. Jonah had not yet regained his full strength from the times of hunger, and without the much-needed fresh food, or warmth from a strong fire during the long winter nights, he had grown increasingly weaker. That morning he did not come to breakfast. His mother went into the small room built onto the house behind the wall where the stove was. "Jonah," she called, "it is past time to be up."

Jonah moaned and tried to sit up. "Mother, I am so thirsty," he whispered. She fell to her knees beside his bed and took his hand. It was too warm. She reached out with her left hand to rest it on his forehead. It was hot and wet.

"Jonah," she gasped. Then she forced herself to sound calm

and reassuring. "Everything is fine. I will get you some fresh water."

She made the trip to the well as swiftly as she could, but when she returned her son was moaning and tossing on his bedroll. Lifting his head, she held it to her bosom as she fought to get him to drink from the cup of water she held to his lips. Then she wiped his hot body with a cool cloth and wrapped him in a dry blanket while she pulled the damp bedding from his sleeping mat. Soon Jonah lay between warm, dry blankets. He began to shiver, so his mother ran to build a fire in the stove to heat the wall his bed rested against. Next, she grabbed a blanket from her own bedroll and tucked it around her son. Still he shivered, so she wrapped her own arms around him and prayed, "O, Lord, is it my own wicked heart that has wanted too much? I promised thee my son, but that knewest I coveted him for myself. Without him I would be alone, but still I promised him to thee. Please forgive my sin. It was the weakness of a mother's heart. Do not hold him to blame! I ask that thou dost not let him perish!" She was sobbing quietly in a corner where she would not startle Jonah, when she heard sounds and knew Elijah had returned with more wood for a fire.

She rushed into the other room, where the prophet stood staring in bewilderment at the fire. "Is my labor of no value that you build a fire without cause?" he asked when she entered.

"It is to warm the wall against which my son lies," the widow explained hastily. Grabbing his hand and pulling him toward the small room, she added, "He is ill! Come quickly."

Elijah went to the lad and touched his hot, feverish brow. Jonah tossed and groaned, but did not open his eyes. Though his body was wet from the fever, he still shivered. His mother began to wipe his face again.

"I will get my blanket," Elijah offered and left the room.

Even with the added blanket, Jonah did not seem to shiver less. All day his mother tended him, with Elijah rushing to bring whatever she asked for, but mostly it was she who ran to the well for fresh water or made cakes, hoping to entice her son to eat. She did not know what to do, and action was the only thing that kept her fear in check. When evening came she was exhausted.

"Go lie down for a while and I will sit with him," Elijah said.

Meekly she obeyed, going to her own room where she rolled out her bed mat and lay down on it, still disheveled from the day. The light that entered through a small window in Jonah's room became dimmer and dimmer as the sun set and the cloudless night wrapped the city in a soft darkness. For the next several hours Elijah tended the boy, wiping his brow with a cool cloth, holding him close when he shook violently, and trying to force water between his pale lips. Yet each time Elijah held Jonah, he could feel the boy growing weaker and his breath becoming shallower as the thin body labored to breathe.

It was deep into the night when a deeper shadow entered the room, passing before the window where the light of the moon had slipped in. The young mother had returned. She looked at the figure bent over the body of her son that lay too still.

"Tell me," she whispered.

"He is gone."

Suddenly, she wailed and ran toward the frail body that no longer expanded with breath. Grabbing her son to her, she spun on the man in the room who had risen and stepped back. "What have I to do with thee?" Her voice became bitter. "O, thou man of God. Have you come to us only to slay my son?" She was nearly incoherent in her grief. "Is it my sin that I loved him too much?" She collapsed onto the small bed, still gripping the limp body to her bosom, and sobbed.

Elijah started to retreat but then touched the woman's shoulder. "God does not punish you," he said. "You have been faithful. Give me your son." His voice was the commanding voice of a prophet.

Weakly, she raised her head and relaxed her grip. Elijah lifted her son into his arms.

"I know that if it is God's will, you can save him," she said pleadingly. Then she covered her face with her hands and sobbed.

Elijah carried the body, which was wrapped in blankets and hanging lifelessly from his arms, out of her house, then crossed to the shed where his room was. Carrying him up the wooden ladder to his loft was difficult. With his left hand he would grasp the left-side support pole, worn smooth from years of use, and step upward with his left foot. Then he would pull himself up to the next rung while his right arm held tight to his precious burden.

In the loft, he walked across the creaking boards and laid Jonah upon his own bed. Then he raised his arms to the heavens, and while gazing through a window at the cold, brilliant stars in the sky, cried aloud, "O Lord, my God, hast thou also brought grief upon the widow with whom I sojourn, by slaying her son?"

Then he stretched himself out upon the body of the child and cried, "O Lord my God, I pray thee, let this child's soul come into him again!" The room was as still as the sky above. Elijah stood up; he had heard the sound of a door opening. The widow had entered the courtyard behind her house. He cast himself upon the boy's inert form and again prayed, "O Lord my God, I pray thee, let this child's soul come into him again!" He heard her footsteps stop below and her hand upon the door to the shed. Again he sprang up. He stuck his head out of the small window and saw her standing below in the moonlight. She did not move; she seemed frozen there at the door to the shed. Tears poured from Elijah's eyes. Stepping quickly back to the bed, he again stretched himself upon the young boy and with great pleading spoke to his maker, "O Lord, my God, I pray thee, let this child's soul come into him again!"

Elijah felt the small chest expand beneath him and heard a small gasp from the boy's lips. Elijah lifted himself off and grabbed the boy's hand. Slowly, the breathing increased, the color ebbed back into Jonah's face, and his hand began to warm in the grasp of the older man.

"I'm thirsty," a small voice said.

"Then let's get you back to your mother and a drink of water."

As Elijah lifted the boy into his arms, Jonah turned to him. "Why am I here?"

"I brought you here."

Carefully, the old man carried the child down the ladder. It was a slow descent, as the strength had gone from the prophet, but he held tight to the still-weak boy in his arms.

The young mother was no longer below. She had lost courage, though not hope, and had returned to her house, where she was sitting silently in the dark. Elijah kicked the partially closed door until it swung open before him. Then he entered the room and moved toward the sitting figure.

"See," he said, handing her the boy, "thy son liveth."

Jonah struggled to sit up on her lap. "Mother, I am thirsty."

She laughed. She cried. She held him so close that she soon felt him struggling to breathe. She laughed again. Then she turned her head toward Elijah. "Now by this I know that thou art a man of God, and that the word of the Lord in thy mouth is truth. Forgive my doubts."

"The Lord loves you, daughter," Elijah said softly. Then he left to drag himself off to his bed in his loft, where he collapsed and slept until the sun was high.

The next day, Elijah and the widow sat down with Jonah and related to him what had occurred. He sat silently listening. Finally he asked, "Was it Elijah's prayer or his power as a prophet that brought me back to life?"

"As a prophet, I am able to exercise the power of God, but it was his will that you returned." Elijah had leaned forward, resting his elbows on his knees and peered earnestly into the young boy's face. "He has a great work for you to do yet."

"If I study hard, will I have this power some day?" Jonah asked.

Elijah sat up and chuckled. "You must study hard, but this power is not earned. It is given to those who have lived worthy of it that God chooses. And remember, it was his will, the power I have, and one other thing." Elijah turned to where the young widow sat. "It was also your mother's faith and goodness that brought you back to life."

Later, while Jonah was resting in the sun behind the house, he thought about what had happened. There were many who believed in other gods. There was a shrine to Astarte in another part of the town. But he had never heard of a miracle such as this being done in the name of Astarte or any of the Gods of the Phoenicians, Assyrians, Egyptians, or Philistines. Jonah had been taught that these were all false gods, and he was not sure how many there were in the world. Sometimes he had wondered how he was to know that the god of his father, of his grandfather, and of Elijah was the only true God. When the miracle of the meal and oil had happened, he had been impressed, but not convinced. His mother might have miscalculated, or Elijah might have brought some with him unseen.

But they claimed that last night he had died. Perhaps he had just been unconscious, but that answer left him cold and empty. It felt like something more had happened than just a swift recovery from being very ill.

Jonah realized the time had come that he could no longer continue without knowing in his own heart if what they testified was true. He dropped to his knees beneath an olive tree that was beginning to bud in a misguided hope of rain. He bowed his head, and with the awkwardness of a boy's first spoken prayer, he asked, "O Jehovah, Creator of the earth and" —he paused, trying to recall the words of other's prayers— "and all things thereon." Jonah took a deep breath. "I ask thee, is it true that I died?" He paused, but there was nothing. "Is it true that because of the power of Elijah and the faith of my mother that I live today?"

He had nothing else to ask. He kept his head bowed and eyes closed for a long time. Finally, Jonah sat up and opened his eyes. The olive tree had not changed. The goat shed where Elijah slept was still in the northern corner of the yard. The spring sunshine still shone down, warming the stone beneath Jonah's bare toes. But slowly the warmth spread through him, and his whole being felt as if angels were embracing him. And Jonah knew.

For everything there is a season,
And a time for every matter under heaven:
A time to be born, and a time to die;
A time to plant, and a time to pluck up what is planted . . .
A time to embrace, And a time to refrain from embracing;
A time to seek, and a time to lose . . .
A time for war, and a time for peace.

Ecclesiastes 3:1–8

Chapter Two

～～～～～～～～～～～～～～～～

*O*ne morning when the famine had stretched into its third year, Elijah came into the house with his daily armful of sticks, and after depositing them beside the stove, sat down for breakfast.

"It is time for me to go to Samaria to talk to King Ahab," he said.

The widow was about to place his breakfast cake on a plate before him. She stopped short, then, composing herself, she set the plate down and returned to get Jonah's.

"Will you be leaving soon?" She tried to steady her voice against the panic she felt. The prophet had brought peace, food, and the power of God to her home.

"I will not leave you without help," he replied. "Where is the boy's father's family?"

"He was of Gath-hepher. His parents and brothers live there if all is well."

"Will you consider taking him to his father's family to

continue his education?"

"I have considered it. I had no means to get there, though," she answered. "I am willing to go for my son."

"Then I will travel with you to Gath-hepher and we will find your husband's family together."

The young woman smiled, feeling a burden lift from her heart. With the prophet promising to be a travel companion, she would no longer worry about the details.

Still, it was several days untile she felt they were ready to depart—until she could leave her home and the village of her childhood behind her. It was the second time she was faced with the parting, the first being at her marriage, but this time there were no parents to say goodbye to, and her sisters had left years earlier. She had no brothers.

There was no money for a donkey, so Elijah and Jonah each shouldered a pack and basic supplies, while the young mother carried a travel-sized jar of the precious meal on her back. They left Zarephath by the southern gate toward the seaport city of Tyre.

They traveled along the sea coast, stopping for the night in towns along the way, and finding hospitality given freely when they offered to provide the whole supper from their supply of meal. At Acco, with a view of Mount Carmel in the distance to the south, they headed east through the Valley of Iphtahel, north of the Jazreel Valley, toward the Sea of Chinnereth. In the fertile hills west of the sea was the village of Gath-hepher.

Entering Gath-hepher, the young widow took the lead, guiding them through the streets to the home where her husband's parents lived. She had lived with her husband in a home not far away before he had died, but she did not go there. His father's house was large with a wall around it that stretched along the street. There was a small window above the gate, indicating a chamber in the wall built above the front portico. They entered the gate, crossed the covered porch where the roof was pierced by steps leading to the upper chamber, and stood at the door, footsore and weary.

Elijah called at the door, and Jonah shifted his pack. He glanced at his mother, who stood beside him, behind the prophet, silent and with much of her face shadowed by her head covering. A young man came to the door.

"Greetings, strangers," he said with reserve. "Please come in."

They slipped off their travel sandals and entered the house. The room began to fill as curious members of the household came to see the visitors. An older man helped his silver-haired wife to a chair. There was a rosy-cheeked, smiling mother with a baby in her arms and two children hiding among her skirts.

Elijah helped the young widow remove the jar from her back that contained the meal that never failed. Jonah also removed his pack and helped Elijah with his. Then Elijah spoke to the room of people. "This is the wife of Amittai and his son, Jonah."

Immediately, the scene became one of rejoicing, as the members of the house rushed forward with open arms and cries of happiness. The two souls from Zarephath were no longer isolated citizens of a village; they were part of a family again. Elijah did not explain who he was, and the widow knew he did not wanted to be delayed by people in the village who would desire to come to see the prophet. He left two days later, following the Jordan River Valley south until he headed west to Samaria.

Jonah had many teachers now: his grandfather and two uncles. The first uncle was the husband of the woman who had three children, who taught lessons when he was not busy in the groves and fields, and the second was the young man who had answered the door, but his time away from the fields was rare and his patience with books was limited. Much of Jonah's day was spent studying, learning, and reciting the commandments, ordinances, statutes, admonitions, precepts, decrees, and words of God. There was always so much more he needed to learn, yet he found it fascinating and he delighted in those hours when he could pore over the scrolls of his grandfathers.

It was common, as the sun set for the day, to find Jonah immersed in his studies, such as land-use regulations within the behavioral laws, or the ceremonial laws regarding sacrifices. His mother would enter the room and ask if he had done his evening chores, and Jonah would admit that he had not been outside since morning. Then his mother would insist that he remember it was also his duty, and a show of appreciation to his grandfather, to spend time helping on the farm.

Despite the drought, through irrigation and hard work, the home of Jonah's grandfather had been able to maintain smaller but productive fields. Jonah loved being part of a larger household. He was given a room to share with two younger cousins, and they would often play together in the evenings when it was too dim to study. On the farm, Jonah learned to work the spillways on the terraced hillsides, to press olives, and to herd and milk goats. His grandfather had been prosperous before the drought, and he still had a dozen goats and various other livestock and chickens.

When people came to Gath-hepher from Samaria, Jonah would clamor among the crowd to hear the news of the capital. He especially thrilled to hear of Elijah. It was this way he heard of Elijah's visit to King Ahab and the prophet's contests on Mount Carmel. A man in a dusty gray robe stood upon the wall around the well that served those whose homes did not have a well, and there the man told the story.

"When Elijah finally consented to appear before Ahab, who has been looking for him throughout Israel, the king asked the prophet, 'Art thou he that troubleth Israel?' Then Elijah stepped toward the king and said, 'I have not troubled Israel, but thou, and thy father's house, in that ye have forsaken the commandment of the Lord, and thou hast followed Baalim.'"

The people clustered around the well nodded their heads. There had been many who had forsaken the Lord because of the choices of the king, and now they were experiencing a drought because of the wickedness in the land. The man in the gray robe continued: "So Elijah challenged Ahab to bring 450 prophets of Baal and four hundred prophets from the grove to Mount Carmel to an altar they had built there. Elijah insisted that all the people were invited to attend. The day was chosen and the people climbed Mount Carmel early in the morning before the sun had begun to rise. And after the multitude had gathered at the altar, with the 950 representatives of the false deities, Elijah stood on a high spot and shouted to the people, 'How long halt ye between two opinions? If the Lord be God, follow him; but if Baal, then follow him.'"

There was silence in the area around the well where the man stood. The people of Gath-hepher felt they had heard the words of Elijah themselves. Indeed, it was time for Israel to choose!

"And that is what happened on the mountain," the man continued after a significant pause. "There was silence. The people had no answer."

He jumped down and sat on the edge of the wall around the well and indicated for the people to sit also. There was a brief stirring, but when everyone was situated he continued his story.

"Then Elijah spoke again to the people, reminding them that although there were nearly one thousand other prophets there representing Baal, only he was there as prophet of the Lord. Then he instructed the priests to choose two bullocks–one for themselves, and one for Elijah to dress. They were to chop their bullock in pieces and lay it on wood, but not to light a fire underneath, and Elijah would dress his and then also lay it on wood, but put no fire underneath.

"Then Elijah instructed, 'Call ye on the name of your gods, and I will call on the name of the Lord, and the God that answers by lighting the fire under our offerings, that we will accept as God.' And the people agreed saying, 'It is well spoken.'

"So the prophets of Baal dressed and cut up their bullock and began to pray, saying, 'O Baal, hear us.' It was still morning and they prayed for hours until noon, but there was no change. The multitude became restless. They were breaking out food from their packs if they brought any, and some were beginning to wander back down the path. The priests became desperate and leaped onto the alter, screaming, 'O Baal, hear us!'

"Then Elijah came closer to where they were ranting and called out loud enough for the people to hear, 'Cry louder, for maybe he is either talking to someone or maybe he is pursuing someone.'"

A chuckle rippled through the crowd gathered around the well at Gath-hepher. The man in the gray robe smiled and continued. "You can imagine how the prophets of Baal felt when the multitude on the mountain began to laugh. They were paying attention now, but not to the priests so much as to Elijah's torment of them. Then Elijah taunted the false prophets again, "Perhaps your god is on a journey." The laughter was spontaneous and interrupted the story again, but the man continued. "Or peradventure he sleepeth, and must be awaked."

Again the crowd laughed. One woman called toward the storyteller, "No, did he really say that to them?"

The man assured her that these were the words of Elijah. Then he continued the story, explaining that the frustrated prophets of Baal began to cut themselves. He told how midday passed and that it was nearly time for the evening sacrifice and still there had been no answer from their god—neither a voice, nor any sign that he had regarded them.

"The multitude had thinned and were again getting restless," the man related. "Then as evening closed in, Elijah stepped forward and had the people come and gather around him and his sacrifice. Away from the altar of Baal was a broken and forgotten altar to the Lord. Elijah had repaired the altar, using twelve stones, and he had built a trench about the altar. Then he placed the wood and took his bullock that had been cut into pieces and laid him on the wood. He turned to the people and asked them to fill four barrels with water and pour it on the sacrifice."

There was a collective gasp that the storyteller ignored. "Then Elijah instructed the people to do it a second time. And when the people on the mountain were beginning to voice their opinions at his folly, he had them do it a third time. The water ran off the bullock and round about the altar, and then Elijah had them fill the trench also with water. Then Elijah stood before the altar and prayed, 'Lord God of Abraham, Isaac, and of Israel, let it be known this day that thou art God in Israel, and that I am thy servant, and that I have done all these things at thy word. Hear me, O Lord, hear me, that this people may know that thou art the Lord God, and that thou hast turned their hearts back again to thee.'

"Then suddenly the fire of the Lord fell from the sky!" The young man abruptly stood up and raised his hands above his head. The crowd around him moved back. "It consumed the burnt sacrifice, and the wood, and the stones, and the dust, and licked up the water that was in the trench!"

There was a stunned silence as the people digested his words. After a moment, Jonah asked, "Everything burned up?"

"Everything on the altar of the Lord, but the altar built to Baal remained untouched. And when the people saw it, they fell on their faces and confessed, 'The Lord, he is the God. The Lord, he is the God.'"

Jonah felt the thrill of wonder and felt the Spirit coursing through him, testifying of the events. When the people dispersed, Jonah lingered and asked the man to repeat the story. Then, after hearing the tale again, and sure that he had the details correct, Jonah, who had been raised from the dead by this same prophet that confronted the priests of Baal, laughed to himself, then went home to tell his mother, his grandfather, and the rest of the household of the miracle.

Immediately after Elijah's contest with the false prophets, and after the false prophets were slain, Elijah had turned to Ahab and said, "Get thee up, go eat and drink, for there is a sound of abundance of rain." And that day, what began as a small cloud over the sea grew to fill the sky with dark thunderclouds that overcame Ahab, who raced for shelter, and he was caught in the deluge before his chariot could get to the Valley of Jazreel.

The rain had fallen in great torrents of deliverance. The thirsty earth had drunk deeply, opening its dry crevices like raspy throats eager for water. The rain filled the land and overflowed, creating rivulets and streams where there had been only animal tracks or drifts of dry earth after a wind. Within days the land of Israel was green and growing again. By the end of the summer, all the people and their livestock had gained strength and energy as their flesh began to cover the sharp edges of their bones, and children began to thrive and run about again.

The years slipped away. There were the years when Syria waged war against Israel, but was defeated. Then the king of Judah came up to Israel, and together the two countries prepared to go to war against Syria. It had been three years of monarchs posturing and retaliating, of famines and sieges, boys going to war but not returning, and crops being planted only to be raided or trampled by armies.

Ramoth-gilead was a city of refuge. When the king of Syria refused to return the city to Israel as he had agreed to do in a signed covenant, Ahab, king of Israel, determined to take it from him. He called in his advisors, his soothsayers, and the false prophets of the various gods. They each told him to go to Ramoth-gilead and fight, that their god would give him the victory. But when Jehoshaphat, king of Judah, heard of the reassuring promises of these prophets of false gods, he asked if there was not a prophet of the Lord to be found. Ahab admitted that there was one, and he had Micaiah brought before them. When Micaiah was brought, the messenger warned him to prophesy good to the king.

"What the Lord saith unto me," Micaiah had responded, "that will I speak."

Then Micaiah was led into the great ivory and gold hall of the palace at Samaria, the capital of Israel. When Ahab saw him, he waved his hand as if what Micaiah said would be of no concern to him, and said, with a suppressed yawn, "Micaiah, shall we go against Ramoth-gilead to battle, or shall we forbear?"

Micaiah looked directly at the king and answered what the king wanted to hear, but in such a way that the king would know it was not a prophecy, "Go, and prosper: for the Lord shall deliver it into the hand of the king." With that Micaiah turned and began to walk from the hall.

However, because Jehoshaphat was present and because Ahab knew that Micaiah was not being truthful, he adjured the prophet to speak the truth, whereupon Micaiah turned, squared his shoulders, and warned King Ahab that the battle would bring his death and that his people would be scattered, like "sheep that have not a shepherd."

It did not change Ahab's determination to wage war against Syria. He was an arrogant man, and since he'd already announced that he was going to war, he would not consider an alternative. He had long allowed the false religions of his wife, Jezebel, to thrive within Israel, and he had come to trust the flattering promises of their priests and prophets. He had only asked Micaiah to prophesy to appease King Jehoshaphat.

Nevertheless, a lingering misgiving caused him to disguise himself as a common soldier. He rode with Jehoshaphat at the front of the combined armies to Ramoth-gilead, but when the battle began, he dropped in among the throngs of soldiers who drove chariots.

Before the battle began, the Syrian king, Ben-hadad, commanded his 32 chariot captains to seek out the king of Israel and kill him. They searched among the prominent captains and rode to where a king was with his chariot in the rear, but they were disappointed to only discover Jehoshaphat, king of Judah. Nevertheless, an errant arrow shot in the battle struck Ahab in a joint of his armor and fatally wounded him, fulfilling the word of the Lord through the prophet Micaiah. The wicked legacy of Ahab was well established, though; the wicked worship of gods that demanded human sacrifice, most often children, and the worship that thrived on sexual sins, was now the chosen theology of Israel.

Then Ahab's son, Ahaziah, began to reign over Israel in Samaria. Unfortunately, like his father, he "did evil in the sight of the Lord," worshipping Baal and offering sacrifices to the false god, continuing the evil practices brought to Israel by his mother, Jezebel, and endorsed by his father.

After Ahab's death, Moab declared its independence and refused to continue to send tribute to Israel. To add to the troubles of the new king, one day Ahaziah fell through the lattice surrounding a balcony at his palace in Samaria and was seriously injured. However, instead of turning to the Lord, he sent messages to the temple of Baalzebub to ask whether he would recover.

Elijah intercepted the messengers and told them that because Ahaziah had chosen to inquire of a pagan god rather than the Lord, Ahaziah would never leave his bed and would soon die. When Elijah's words were fulfilled, Jehoram, Ahaziah's brother, became the new king. Ahaziah had reigned only two years. However, the new king, Jehoram, continued the wicked, immoral practices that took place in the pagan temples and groves.

Because of Moab's rebellion, Judah joined Israel and Edom—which was under servitude to Israel— in a campaign against Moab. Because they followed the advice of the prophet Elisha, the three armies were successful. When the king of Moab saw that his army was being defeated and that he was trapped, he took seven hundred soldiers in an attempt to flee the city, but the hosts of the Edomites drove him back. So he took his eldest son, his heir, and offered him for a burnt offering to Chemosh, the pagan god of the Moabites. When it was evident that the Moabites were again subjugated, Israel returned home, but not to peace.

Fear not: for they that be with us are more than they that be with them.

2 Kings 6:16

Chapter Three

⊙⌒⊙⌒⊙⌒⊙⌒⊙⌒⊙⌒⊙⌒⊙⌒⊙⌒⊙⌒⊙

With a chopping stroke, Jonah wedged the ax into the piece of timber that stood on its end. Then, with the ax imbedded in the piece of wood, he slammed the wood downward onto the stump that held it, driving the ax through and splintering the piece into two smaller ones. These he picked up and tossed into a nearby pile he would stack later.

Jonah was a man now, though still young. He was steadying another piece of wood when a voice spoke from behind him. "May peace be upon you."

Jonah turned to face a middle-aged man who stood with his hands clasped in front of him. "Peace to you," Jonah answered.

When the man did not move or speak further, Jonah offered him a seat on a large piece of chopped wood and went to get him a drink from a nearby water vessel. Soon, Jonah returned and handed the man the cup of water, then pulled up another large piece of wood that he stood on its end.

The man accepted the cup, and when he had drained it, he held it out to Jonah. "My name is Elisha."

Recognizing the name, Jonah stumbled in his step to retrieve the cup.

"Come, sit beside me and tell me of your studies," Elisha directed.

"How do you know of me?" Jonah asked, awed by the prophet's presence.

Elisha smiled. "Your first teacher told me of you."

"Elijah!" Jonah gasped. He had almost come to believe that the experiences of his childhood had never occurred. "I wish I could have seen him again!"

Elisha did not respond, so Jonah tried to calm his enthusiasm. "I have studied much," he said, trying to sound casual, as if he conversed with a prophet every day. "This is my grandfather's home, and he planned for me to take over his household. But my uncles are better prepared for that, and though I am strong, I am more of a scholar."

"How will you support your family?" Elisha asked.

"I will take my mother to live with me when my house is built. My first uncle has arranged for me to have a small farm. The foundation is laid and a well is dug. It will be a small farm, but it will be sufficient."

Then Jonah saw Elisha looking at him intently and realized he had inferred more. "I do not have a wife yet," Jonah said.

"It is nearly time."

Jonah did not respond, but he managed to close his lower jaw after an awkward moment.

Then Elisha laughed. "But first, I would like you to travel with me. I have come to ordain you to the priesthood of God."

Jonah was overwhelmed with this new turn his life was

taking, and yet it felt as if he had been on this path all along. Two days later he had packed, put his duties in order, and left to travel with the prophet. He followed Elisha where Elisha felt inclined to go. Elisha filled their travels with tales, causing the long, dusty miles to go by quickly. He told Jonah of the time he helped a widow pay her debt by multiplying her oil. He told Jonah of the woman who had no children and how after his promise of a child she conceived and bore a son, but when the son was older he died. Then Elisha, as Elijah had done, brought the son back to life. He told of making bitter, inedible food good again and of feeding many with a few loaves of barley bread and a few ears of corn, an act that foreshadowed a greater miracle that would be performed more than once in another eight hundred years by one who was greater than a prophet. However, the story Jonah enjoyed most was the story of Naaman, who was healed of leprosy. And in all his tales, Elisha taught Jonah that the Lord can do all things for those that have faith and believe. But Elisha also warned that the power of God was not for profit or sale, the prophet explaining how his old servant, Gehazi, had attempted to profit from Naaman's miracle.

Elisha also told Jonah of the many times the king of Syria had sent armies against the king of Israel. But Elisha had advised the king, and when the king hearkened to his words, Israel had been the victor.

One evening Elisha and Jonah arrived in Dothan, a city located a few miles north of Samaria. The city was built on the flat top of a hill that had steep sides. The road up the hill cut back and forth until it arrived at the gate at the summit. Elisha found lodging for them in the home of a family with which Elisha had lodged with in the past. The home was built against the city wall, and the room given Elisha and Jonah was built on the roof of the house. It had a view beyond its door, over the city wall at the Dothan Valley to the west and the hills of Samaria directly below and beyond.

Jonah rose early the next morning; the bright rays of the morning sun had come in through the door of their room and awakened him. After he had washed in preparation for his morning prayers, he heard a distant noise that was unlike the usual sounds of an awakening city. He left the room by the rooftop door and went to the wall to see what caused the noise. It came from outside the city wall, at the base of the hill.

The sun was just rising over the hills to the east, and some of its rays caught the glint of metal below and flashed upward to where Jonah stood. He squinted and could see that in the dust and the short-cropped grasses of the plain was camped a host of Syrian soldiers, including horses and chariots. The massive army completely encompassed the city. Jonah rushed back inside the rooftop room to the mat where Elisha slept. Gripping Elisha's shoulders, Jonah shook him. "Master," he called, "come, the Syrians have arrived in the night and their army is upon us!" Jonah led the way to the wall and Elisha followed, wrapping his mantle around himself. Jonah waited until he had seen the army below, then, frustrated by Elisha's calmness, exclaimed, "What are we to do?"

Then Elisha turned to Jonah, carefully laid his hand upon his shoulder, and said in a clear, strong voice, "Fear not, for they that be with us are more than they that be with them." He spread his hand out to indicate the Syrian camp. Thinking that the prophet was still drowsy, Jonah was about to explain the situation more clearly, when Elisha shook his head to stop him.

Then Elisha lifted his eyes toward the sky and called upon God. "Lord, I pray thee, open his eyes that he may see."

Elisha pointed over the wall and Jonah went to look. There Jonah saw that the sides of the whole mountain on which Dothan was built were filled with horses and chariots. They were not of metal, wooden wheels, and leather harnesses, but of fire. A thrill coursed through Jonah's whole body and he stepped back from the view. When he turned to Elisha, the prophet had already dressed and was going to the steps built against the house that led from the roof to the ground. Jonah quickly followed the prophet, feeling like he was a mere observer in a great drama.

He heard Elisha, who had stopped at the base of the steps, pray again, "Lord, smite this people who have come against me, I pray thee, with blindness." There seemed to be a rippling disturbance beyond the wall, and then a slow wailing began that seemed to grow.

Elisha hurried toward the city gate. The keepers of the gate, who had also seen the host below, refused to open the gate.

"I am Elisha. I have come to speak with the Syrians," the prophet declared.

"We have alerted the city, and soon the guards will be with us," they explained.

"Your guards will not be sufficient. Besides, it is me that they have come for. Open the gate."

This time the guard obeyed without further protest.

Once beyond, Elisha began to descend down the road that led to the host below. Jonah followed uncertainly, but the guards remained within the walls of the city and mounted the gate tower for a better view. When Elisha was within twenty feet of the bottom, he called out, "Where is your captain? Why have you come against this city?"

Then the host, still in chaos from their blindness, quieted a bit, and Elisha repeated his questions. After more confused conversation among themselves, one solider called back, "Who are you? We have been blinded and cannot see what we seek."

"What do you seek that you come upon us in the night?" Elisha called.

"We are looking for Elisha, who serves the king of Israel, and we have been informed that he would be in Dothan."

Then Elisha cried out, "This is not the place you seek. Perhaps your guide became lost in his blindness. But if you follow me, I will bring you to the man whom ye seek."

Then he turned to Jonah and spoke softly, "Ride to Samaria and have the king prepare his army to surround these Syrians when I lead them to him."

So that day Elisha, after careful arrangement of horses and leads, and with the help of the men of Dothan, led the hosts from Syria to Samaria, where the army of Israel that was at Samaria surrounded them. Then he prayed, "Lord, open the eyes of these men that they may see." And the Lord opened their eyes, and the army looked around and saw that they were in the midst of their enemy.

Then Jehoram, king of Israel, asked Elisha if he should have his men fall upon the Syrians and smite them, but Elisha answered, "Do not smite them, for they are captives. Give them bread and water, then release them to return to their own country."

Then Jehoram did as Elisha said, and when the host had eaten and drunk, he sent them away without their weapons, and the host departed in a great cloud of dust, confused but grateful.

Now when Ben-hadad, king of Syria, heard the story from his captains and the power they had experienced from the God of Israel, the king determined that he would no longer attempt secret attacks on Israel, nor would he trouble to waste more effort on Elisha, but that he would confront Israel in open warfare. So Ben-hadad gathered his entire host and went up to lay siege to Samaria.

But Elisha sent Jonah away and promised to come visit him soon at his home in Gath-hepher. And so it was secondhand that Jonah heard of the great siege of Samaria and the miraculous deliverance of food left by the retreating enemy. This time he was not astounded as he heard of the part Elisha had played.

As he sat around his fire at home in the evenings, Jonah often reflected on his time spent with Elisha. He recalled the story of the woman who desired a child and the faith that it taught. Many of Elisha's stories were about faith. The very toil of traveling with Elisha had taught Jonah patience and endurance. He could recall many principles that Elisha taught him, whether from stories or example. However, this last experience with Elisha confused Jonah. The manifestation of the army of fire had showed Jonah the power that was available to God's prophet, and yet Elisha had not exercised a righteous judgment upon the Syrian army, but had been merciful toward them. Had not Elijah had the prophets of Baal and of the grove slain? Why had Elisha spared the enemy that had come in the night to kill him? Jonah decided he would ask Elisha when they met again, not realizing that when that time did come he would not even think of it. It was a lesson Jonah had yet to learn.

One evening, Jonah sat by the fire with his mother, who was beginning to slow with age. Carefully sewing a new tunic for Jonah, she held the work close to the light from the fire and bent over it so that she could see it clearly. "Jonah," she said, "I desire to hold my grandchild before I die."

Jonah was taken aback. "Mother," he spoke gently,

reaching for her hand, "You do not have a grandchild. I am not married."

"That is the problem, but time is running out, so I have taken care of that. Your uncle has been to see the elders of the village, and one of them has a granddaughter whom I would like you to meet. It is true that she is getting a bit older, but then you do not have a large farm or trade to offer. However, your home is nearly built and it is time."

"Mother!" Jonah finally interrupted. "You have found a girl you want me to take for a wife?"

"That is what I said." She smiled patiently. "They will be coming here for the Sabbath meal tonight."

Jonah was speechless. Later, when he bathed for the Sabbath, he realized that he felt nervous. Once again he combed his hair, which his mother had trimmed that afternoon, and then he thought to trim his beard. Jonah was a strong, handsome young man, but his mother was right. What did he have to offer as a husband? Then he remembered his mother had said the girl was not as young as many brides. What did that mean? Was the girl in her seventeenth or even nineteenth year? Since he was in his mid-twenties, what did it matter? He was not concerned about age.

That evening as the sun set, Jonah walked into the room where his uncle presided at the head of the table, now that his grandfather was gone. His mother waited to light the two candles that signified their commitment as a people to observe and remember. He took his place beside his younger uncle, who had married four years ago and was now the father of two, while the elder one now had five children. Yes, it was time for Jonah to take a wife.

The girl came into the room behind her mother and her father. She was tall, but she kept her head lowered, so her head

covering hung forward, hiding her face. Jonah missed much
of what was said until he heard her father introduce her. "This
is Freda." Jonah instantly made the mental connection. *Joy.*
Her name meant joy. He could not take his eyes from the void
where her face hid. Then for the briefest moment, while his
uncle recited over the cup of wine, she lifted her head. A glow
from a nearby candle shone directly between the folds of her
head covering and he saw her perfect face. She had large, dark
eyes and a kind, full mouth. It happened in an instant and then
her face dropped. But in that moment, Jonah had looked into
her eyes and felt she would bring him happiness.

Because signing the contracts would entail writing, this
would not be done until after Sabbath, but the day of the
wedding was set, and all too soon the evening was over. Jonah
watched Freda's tall, thin form as she moved to exit the room.
At the door, she stopped and lifted her head once more. It was
as if she knew exactly where Jonah was standing. She looked
at his beard rather than make eye contact again, but she smiled,
and a playful dimple appeared in her left cheek. Then she was
gone. Jonah would not see her again until they were married,
because she was going to visit her sister who lived near the sea
coast and was about to deliver her fourth child.

"If Ammon and Moab must reign in the land
Thou gavest thine Israel, fresh from thy hand . . ."
Whose God will ye serve, O ye rulers of men?
Will ye build you new shrines in the slave-breeder's den?

Oliver Wendell Holmes

Chapter Four

Jonah had been married five years when Elisha visited again. Freda had served a delicious supper, then gathered their young son into her arms to carry him off to bed.

"Kiss Papa," the boy called with his arms outstretched. His mother paused at the base of the ladder, and Jonah stepped across the room to take him from Freda.

"I'll be just a moment," Jonah said to Elisha, who sat comfortably by a fire. Then he placed his son on his shoulders and mounted the ladder, followed by his wife, whose belly was beginning to show the roundness of another child that would be born after the harvest.

When Jonah returned, Elisha was standing. "The Lord has sent me to anoint you as a prophet. He has a mission for you."

Jonah stared in wonder, but when Elisha insisted that he was sincere, Freda was called and placed in a chair near the fire. Then Jonah sat in a chair and Elisha placed his hands on his head. When the ordination was completed, the two prophets embraced as tears ran down Jonah's cheeks. Then he held out his arm for his wife, who slipped in under his shoulder, her own tears flowing.

"What would the Lord have me do?" Jonah asked.

Elisha indicated for them to sit again. He leaned forward, his elbows on his knees and his hands clasped in front of him. "Ahab and Jezebel have left a great sin upon Israel. Their sons continue the evil practices, and the people are deceived. The Lord would have you travel to Ramoth-gilead, on the border with Syria. There you will find a man named Jehu, son of Jehoshaphat the son of Nimshi. He is a captain of the army of Israel."

Elisha reached toward a nearby table and picked up the box that contained the oil he had used to anoint Jonah. "Take this," Elisha said, "and anoint Jehu to be king over Israel."

Jonah swallowed. Anointing another man to usurp the current king was not a simple task.

"Years ago," Elisha said, "Elijah told me this was to be. The time has come that Jehu has the position and the respect for this to happen. Take Jehu away from his brethren, though, and go into a private chamber. Then when you are done, do not tarry, but return home to the safety of your family."

The next day Elisha accompanied Jonah on the first part of his journey. They traveled first to the southern shore of the Sea of Chinnereth, where they made camp along the shore and feasted on bread from their packs and on sardines they bought from a local fisherman. The next day, they traveled in the relatively smoother terrain of the hills overlooking the Jordan River, going down to shore for fresh water at noon. They traveled down the river until the point where Jonah was to cross the river to follow the road east to Ramoth-gilead.

They camped there that night, and the next day Jonah hired a boat to take him across the river. Elisha would continue south and then turn west toward Samaria. Each would arrive at his destination before nightfall.

Ramoth-gilead was a city of refuge, an asylum for individuals who had killed a person by negligence but without breaking the law. The road to the city was wide, smooth, and well maintained, so that a refugee could flee there quickly. Like other cities of refuge, Ramoth-gilead was of moderate size—not so small that there could be scarcity of food, which might force refugees to leave the safety of the city in search of sustenance, and not so large that the city could easily hide an "avenger of blood" in the crowds.

Jonah had traveled only a few days from Gath-hepher when he arrived at Ramoth-gilead. Nevertheless, his clothes were dirty from camping out, and he had to explain at the gate that he was not there for asylum, but had come to seek the captain of the army that was stationed within the city.

It was past sunset and the streets were dark, but the building to which Jonah had been directed to was well lit with torches and oil lamps. He entered the open door and pushed aside a heavy drapery. Inside, several soldiers sat at rough wooden tables, while others lounged on the floor. Jonah had learned that they had returned that afternoon from a patrol to the northeast, and they were at various stages of dress after having removed their armor and portions of their uniforms. The men were dirty, smelly, and mostly drunk. The food before them was greasy, and there were piles of discarded bones at each man's elbow. The soldiers' sleeves showed signs of having served as cloths to wipe their faces and their noses.

A serving lad had picked his way between the men, refilling mugs and cups with a golden liquid, and was now returning with an empty pitcher toward the doorway. Jonah reached out and gently gripped his arm.

"Which one is Jehu?" he asked.

Clearly surprised that someone would ask such a question, the boy shrugged and said, "That tall one with the big voice." The boy pointed to a man dressed in the clothing of an officer, with a finer fabric and with golden embroidery on the hem of his tunic. Jehu had removed most of his armor and stood with a large cup in his left hand that he clung to as a soldier might hold a shield, but that Jonah did not see him drink from. With his right hand, Jehu punctuated the words of a song the men around him were singing loudly.

Jonah felt instant misgivings about the man, but when he saw how popular the man was with those who sang with him or that cheered on another song, Jonah reflected that at least Jehu might inspire a loyal following.

Jonah asked the lad to give Jehu a message. The lad shook his head, indicated the empty pitcher, and left the noisy room. Jonah sighed, then began to pick his way through the men. He tried to keep to the perimeter, but men were propped against the wall. As he crossed the room, several soliders pointed to him and whispered. One called out, "Hey innkeeper, where's your pitcher? My cup is empty!" Ignoring the jeer, Jonah approached the captain.

Jehu sat on a long bench with several other captains, and Jonah had to step over two men to stand before the table where he sat. When Jehu looked up at him, Jonah saw confusion cross the man's face.

"Peace to you," he said to Jonah.

"Peace unto you. I have an errand for thee, captain."

Jehu looked to his left and his right, and Jonah realized the captain probably thought he would have to gather his men together immediately and ride out on another campaign. Finally, Jehu asked, "Unto which of us is this errand directed?"

"To thee, O captain," Jonah said, looking directly at Jehu. "Can we go somewhere more private?"

Jehu turned to look again at his companions, and they nodded their heads toward him, indicating that he should go with Jonah.

Jehu arose, scratched at his dark beard, then ordered men to move so that he and Jonah might walk from the room unhindered. The path was immediately cleared, and Jehu led Jonah to the back of the room, where they passed into a smaller one and then out another door. Jehu led Jonah across a small courtyard surrounded by two-story buildings that served as rooms for the soldiers. He went to the far side, where massive stone steps led up to a higher patio. Mounting the steps two at a time, Jehu entered a house built on the higher ground. When he had closed the door behind him, he set down the lamp he had carried with him, illuminating the large room. It was filled with debris and sleeping mats tossed haphazardly aside.

Then he turned to look at Jonah, who cleared his throat and began, "I am Jonah, a prophet. I have been sent by Elisha, who was commissioned by Elijah, to anoint you to be king over Israel."

Jehu's face paled, and he groped for a bench and sat down.

Jonah pulled the box from his pack.

"There is a king over Israel," Jehu replied, clearly stunned. "I serve King Jehoram."

"The king continues the wicked practices of his parents. It is the will of the Lord that a new king lead Israel."

Jehu shook his head. "Why me?"

"Because the Lord has chosen you."

Several more times, Jehu questioned the choice, and each

time Jonah reassured him. Then Jonah poured some of the oil from the box on Jehu's head, placed his hands on his head, and declared, "Thus saith the Lord God of Israel, I anoint thee king over the people of the Lord, even over Israel." Jonah paused, his hands still in place, and then he spoke without hesitation, the words flowing from him. "And thou shalt smite the house of Ahab thy master, that I may avenge the blood of my servants the prophets, and the blood of all the servants of the Lord at the hand of Jezebel. For the whole house of Ahab shall perish.And the dogs shall eat Jezebel, and there shall be none to bury her." The words stopped. Suddenly frightened by what he had just pronounced, Jonah lifted his hands from Jehu's head, then turned and fled from the house, leaving Jehu sitting in the chair.

Beyond the door, on the steps leading down to the courtyard below, Jonah met several of the captains from the hall. He pushed through them, not listening to their entreaties as to his purpose. They were about to detain him, concerned for what he had done, when Jehu came out of the house.

"Is all well?" one man called up to Jehu. "What has this mad man been doing?"

"I thought you knew the man and what his errand was, or I would not have come here with him," Jehu answered.

"We do not know the man," another captain replied. "Tell us what his message was."

So Jehu told them of Jonah's errand, declaring that Jonah had anointed him king over Israel so that he might destroy the posterity of Ahab beginning with Jehoram.

The men, who were loyal to Jehu and discouraged with the practices of Jehoram, immediately removed their cloaks and mantles and cast them at Jehu's feet where he stood at the top of the stairs. Some ran and brought back trumpets such as were blown in battle. They blew the sound for attack and all the men shouted, "Jehu is king of Israel!"

Jonah watched from the corner of a wall that stuck out from the hall. When the proclamation ended, he gathered his robes about him, walked toward the city gate, and began his journey home.

The works of Jehu—how he killed Jehoram and ordered the execution of Jezebel and all the grandsons of Ahab—are written in the book of Kings. Jehu went throughout all of Israel and put a stop to the worship of Baal. And the Lord said to Jehu, through a prophet, "Because thou hast done well in executing that which is right in mine eyes, and hast done unto the house of Ahab according to all that was in mine heart, thy children of the fourth generation shall sit on the throne of Israel." But Jehu did not destroy the golden calves the people worshipped at Bethel and Dan, so the Israelites continued their idol worship, their sin increasing with each king.

Jonah continued as a prophet for the Lord, serving as Elisha asked or as the Lord directed him. During the reign of Jehu's grandson, Jeroboam II, Jonah prophesized to Jeroboam regarding his war campaigns. Although Jeroboam engaged in the wicked practice of worshipping idols and many other practices brought to him from other lands, the Lord used him to further his plan for Israel. When Jonah told Jeroboam that he should restore the northern boundaries of Israel according to the boundaries established by Joshua, the king did so. He recovered cities from Hamath, at the foot of Mt. Hermon in the Lebanon Valley, to Damascus, capital of Syria.

All that Jonah did or advised, even to charging Israel to conquer the armies of the Syrians, enlarging the bounds of the kingdom to the north, was according to the word of the Lord. Jonah came to think of himself as Israel's prophet.

Now the word of the Lord came unto Jonah the son of Amittai, saying, Arise, go to Nineveh, that great city, and cry against it; for their wickedness is come up before me.

Jonah 1:1–2

Chapter Five

~~~~~~~~~~~~~~~~~~~~~~~~~~~~~~~

It was as a dream, and yet the words that thundered through Jonah's mind were clear. He sat up abruptly, shaken from his sleep. He tried to reason that the message had just been a dream. The Lord could not have meant Nineveh, that terrible and feared city deep in the heart of Assyria.

"Better to have me preach to thy people here in Israel!" he said in a hoarse whisper. "This is where I have always served thee. This is thy people. And have not many of thy people forgotten thy ways? Let me cry repentance in Israel." Yet the echo pounded again in his head: "Go to Nineveh, that great city, and cry against it!"

Jonah rose from his bed, dressed, covered his head, and went to a basin to wash his hands three times—first the right and then the left—while reciting, "Modeh Ani li-fa-ne-cha Melech chai ve-ka-yam, she-heche-zar-ta bee nish-ma-tee be-chem-la rabba ehm-una-techa." ("I offer thanks to Thee, living and eternal King, for Thou hast mercifully restored my soul within me; thy faithfulness is great.")

He dried his reddened hands and then moved to his window, which looked southeast toward the temple in far-off Jerusalem, to say his morning prayer. Yet the words of the shacharit were empty this morning, for in his heart the decree of the Lord still vibrated. This was not like the time he traveled to anoint Jehu, or the time he prophesied to Jeroboam. This was a call to go deep into the dark land of his most-feared enemy, and cry repentance to them!

The dawn was spreading its pale blue light across the horizon when his youngest grandchild arrived, bringing fresh milk. Adira often came to help Grandmother Freda with various chores, or to accompany her on her visits to needy families. When Jonah entered the second room of his simple home, Adira was sweeping the hard floors, which were never allowed to gather dust. He stood, amazed at the stillness, realizing that he had almost expected dark clouds and thunderous explosions from heaven to accompany the words in his heart. They had been so clear and forceful. Didn't words from the Lord such as these require a display of twisted lightning and mighty winds?

He sat down at the rough wooden table and gazed out the window at the deep but familiar shadows that began to take the shape of a fig tree, a grindstone, and Freda among the chickens. There was no shaking of the earth or blazing of a falling star; there had been only the words spoken to his mind and to his heart. He closed his eyes and recited the blessing on the morning meal.

The child stood motionless until he had finished praying. As she resumed her sweeping, Jonah asked her, "Adira, what think you of Nineveh?" He barely glanced toward the window from where the early sun had begun to fill the room with light, outlining her simple, brown wool dress, her rough linen overdress, and the dull scarf that tied back her hair.

The child did not raise her eyes but again paused in her sweeping. Then, in a clear voice that gradually became stronger, she answered, "Of Nineveh? That great city of the Assyrians? I have heard it is a very wicked city, where mothers bake bread from the bones of their ancestors, and fathers offer their own children in sacrifice to giant bulls who have the heads of men."

"I have heard similar tales, but perhaps not all such stories are true."

Jonah took a piece of warm barley bread from the polished wooden platter in front of him and, as was the custom, dipped the bread into salt before taking a bite. Minutes passed before he spoke again: "Still, it is a fearsome city. Not a place one would desire to visit." He had forgotten the child and was speaking aloud to himself.

"Indeed!" Now Adira looked directly at her grandfather. She could be quite passionate about her opinions, and her words often amused Jonah. "They say many people are taken as slaves to Nineveh and never return." Her eyes widened. "They say if you are not a citizen of Nineveh, they will not let you pass their gates until you have sworn an oath to worship the terrible beasts that roam among the woods. They say if you do not worship them, you will become lost and wander forever in the forests until you die of hunger."

Jonah took a drink of milk to hide his smile, almost choking as he did so. The child ran for a towel, and as Jonah put down his cup, a shadow fell across his creased face. Taking the towel from Adira's small hand, he wiped the milk from his thick beard, which was mostly gray now. "Still, it is a fearsome city," he repeated softly, thinking of the command he had received.

Jonah began to reason that at his age he deserved a rest. Were there no young prophets available to make the journey to Nineveh? He looked out the window to where his wife was now speaking to a neighbor while laying out wet bedding to dry in the warming sunshine. She draped the bedding over the low roof that covered the feeding trough of their five goats.

Jonah went to a shelf that ran the length of one wall of the room and carefully selected a scroll from the many stacked there. Crossing to the table, he opened it to read from the writings of Moses about Abraham's trip to Egypt, but he found little comfort in it. Abraham had not been commanded to cry repentance to the Egyptians.

Later that morning, Jonah's friend Aziel stopped by, and Jonah invited him to join them for the midday meal. After they had finished the meal and offered a prayer of thanks, Freda quietly cleared the platters from the table. Then she stepped into the garden to retrieve the wool blankets, which were now dry.

Jonah leaned toward his friend, repeating the question he had asked Adira: "What think you of Nineveh?"

"I do not think of Nineveh." It was a simple but faithful answer. One did not think on the wickedness of other nations.

"Do the prophets not say that the children of God will be cut off from their land if they become wicked?" He stared intently into his friend's eyes. "As wicked as many are in Israel today, would God allow another nation, even perhaps the wicked Assyrians, to bring this evil upon us?"

Aziel looked at his younger friend and smiled, then stroked his beard. Jonah waited patiently, knowing that Aziel was searching his mind for a scripture relevant to their conversation.

At last Aziel sat back, his fingers knitted together, and

recited, "'But if ye shall at all turn from following me, ye or your children, and will not keep my commandments and my statutes which I have set before you, but go and serve other gods, and worship them: Then will I cut off Israel out of the land which I have given them; and this house, which I have hallowed for my name, will I cast out of my sight.'"

Aziel licked his lips and paused, but no response came from his friend, so he went on, "It continues, 'And they shall say, Why hath the Lord done thus unto this land, and to this house? And they shall answer, Because they forsook the Lord their God, who brought forth their fathers out of the land of Egypt, and have taken hold upon other gods, and have worshipped them, and served them: therefore hath the Lord brought upon them all this evil.'"

Leaning back against the wall, Aziel challenged Jonah: "There are other prophecies of Israel being cut off from the promises of God. Yet what do the prophets say that leads you to think it could be done by the Assyrians?"

Jonah's intent was not to pleasurably debate the words of the prophets. He sighed and then, as if trying to organize his troubled thoughts, he slowly said, "There are many in Israel who have forgotten the Lord their God, who worship false gods and have set aside his commandments." Jonah stood and began to pace as he spoke, his agitation reflected in his crisply spoken words. "Also, the Assyrians are mighty and could take our people captive from this land which has been given them. Others may battle against us, and if they conquered, they could rule over us. Yet Assyria is large enough to carry the people of Israel away, cutting us off from our land. Is it not so?"

He did not wait for an answer but rather, as in defense of the words of the holy prophets, he rushed on, stopping to stand in front of his friend. "But surely if the Assyrians are wicked, then the Lord will destroy them as well. Did the Lord not also say, 'He that sacrificeth unto any god, save unto the Lord only, he shall be utterly destroyed'?"

Aziel looked curiously at his friend. "He has so promised."

"So if the Assyrians do not repent, they could be destroyed as well." Jonah continued his pacing. "In that case, they would not be a threat to our people. The children of Israel might then repent."

Jonah walked toward the door, looking out to the hills far to the east. "But if the great empire of the Assyrians were to receive a prophet at Nineveh, the city where their king lives much of the year, and if they listened and chose to repent, Assyria would not be destroyed at this time. Then the Lord might allow them to be the means of cutting off his people."

Aziel slowly nodded his head. "This is so," he replied. "It would be a terrible thing for Israel to have the Assyrians come against them." But then Aziel smiled and added, "But why would Nineveh listen to a Hebrew prophet?" He chuckled and reached for a fig.

"Why indeed?" Jonah asked, smiling weakly. "That would be as likely as the dividing of the Red Sea." He turned back to where his friend sat. "Forgive me, Aziel. I did not tell you, but I plan to be gone for a while. Perhaps for many months."

Aziel did not reply at first, but then he looked at Jonah closely. "This is troublesome news." He paused and then continued. "Tell me, my friend who is a prophet of the Lord, do you go to Nineveh?"

"No!" replied Jonah firmly. "I am going the opposite way—to Tarshish."

Explaining to Freda why he was going on a long trip had not been so easy. She had looked at him sharply, then knelt down before him. "My husband, has the Lord called you to Tarshish?"

"No," Jonah answered truthfully. "He has not called me to Tarshish, but I need to go there. I hope to return within the year. They say the ships travel the Way of the Sea once each year. It is still spring, so I will be able to go far before the winter storms set the ships to rest."

From the look in Freda's eyes, Jonah knew she suspected he was not telling her everything. Nevertheless, that he would be gone on a long, perilous journey was all he was going to tell her.

She took his hand and finally asked, "When do you leave, so that I can prepare you to go?"

"Within the week. I will go tomorrow to buy a donkey to ride to Joppa."

His wife stood up and smoothed her skirts, then said, "Jonah, buy one for me too. I will be traveling to Jerusalem."

He looked at her in surprise.

"It is the time of the spring pilgrimage. I will go to offer sacrifice that you will travel safely," she said firmly.

Jonah loved and cherished his wife. She was kind, giving, and intelligent. He could discuss the scriptures with her as well as he could with many of the elders of the village. But she was also unpredictable and strong-willed. He had learned to bend with the winds that blew her from one concern to the next, as long as they did not alter the peace of their home. But at times such as this, she frustrated him. He had not consciously considered what she would do while he was gone, though he had dimly pictured her in their home, continuing to minister to the neighbors and to care for their grandchildren who were near. He could not imagine her taking a journey of her own, especially alone.

"A pilgrimage to Jerusalem is not safe for you to take alone," he said. "I would have you stay here and care for our family."

"Our family is able to care for themselves. I only bother them so that I may be with my grandchildren. But the grandchildren will be fine while I am gone. Besides, I will not go alone. I will travel with Aziel and his wife, who are making the pilgrimage this year. They have made arrangements to travel with several families. I had hoped we could both go."

"Aziel did not mention it when he was here." Jonah frowned, thinking the conversation had taken a strange turn. Then he realized that the new focus diverted his wife from asking further questions about his own upcoming journey, and he felt some relief. "I will ask our son to tend our goats while we are gone. Tomorrow, I will secure two sturdy donkeys."

Jonah opened the door and stepped out into the cool night air before his wife could question him further.

I remember the black wharves and the slips,
And the sea-tides tossing free;
And the beauty and mystery of the ships
And the magic of the sea.

Henry Wadsworth Longfellow

Chapter Six

⁓⁓⁓⁓⁓⁓⁓⁓⁓⁓⁓⁓⁓⁓

The road to Joppa was long and tedious, and Jonah quickly wearied of traveling it. He tried to not worry about his wife's journey alongside the Jordan River Valley. When her party was just north of the Salt Sea, they would turn east toward Jerusalem, the capital of Judah. She would be gone nearly two months. He was partially consoled that one of their older grandsons had gone with her, but in each of his prayers Jonah asked for the Lord to protect her. But whenever he prayed now, he felt hypocritical, since he was blatantly disobeying the Lord's command to go to Nineveh.

Jonah headed southeast toward the sea coast. By the second day, he was sore from riding and sore from walking. That evening he arrived at the outskirts of the city of Dor. Though not as well known for its purple cloth as was Sidon, Dor also harvested the murex shellfish from which the purple dye was extracted.

The sun was setting over the western sea when Jonah neared

the closest of the impressive gates built by the Phoenicians. He stopped. Though assigned to the tribe of Manasseh, Dor had never been claimed, because Joshua's men had been unable to drive the Canaanites out. It was a pagan city, and it might prove difficult for a believer in God to find hospitality within.

Jonah took a deep breath and walked forward, leading the donkey over the well-packed road toward the massive, four-chambered gate that was still open. Incongruous with the scale of the gate, a single guard dosed within the arched passage on a stool, with a brass bowl at his feet. Jonah walked past the first set of chambers to where the guard sat, then nudged the man, whose dirty turban had fallen over his eyes. The guard groaned, his breath caught, and then he settled into a contented snore. His stool was angled against the passage wall, and his feet dangled from the stool, testifying that he was a small man. Against the wall beside him was propped a disproportionately long spear. Jonah peered into the bowl on the ground and saw coins of various denominations and worth. He smiled, added a shiny brass coin, passed the second set of chambers, and entered the city.

The streets were mostly empty, and the soft glow of oil lamps shown from the windows of homes. Jonah imagined the wife of the guard berating him for falling asleep and staying too late again. Then he thought to offer a prayer of gratitude that the guard had still been there and that the gate was still open.

Jonah walked down the main road into the city. Homes of various heights and prominence had been built close together. Over the rooftops he could discern a larger building—probably a temple to the goddess Astarte or some other pagan deity. As Jonah looked for a house he could approach, he saw three houses built together. They had similar features, but the low wall built around each roof separated it from the others, as the law dictated. Jonah smiled. These were the homes of believers. He approached the center one, where the door was ajar. Tradition held that anciently, Abraham and Lot had left the doors of their homes open on all four sides to receive strangers. Jonah tapped on the door, then stepped inside and called a greeting. The ground floor of the home housed a ram in a pen to the side. The rest of the floor was filled with storage jars and cooking implements. The light from the upper floor poured down from the opening above a ladder to the left. A face appeared in the opening. "Good evening," a small boy of about six years greeted Jonah.

"Good evening. I am a stranger in your city and am seeking a place to rest."

"You must come up to supper." the child said brightly. He descended and filled a basin with water for Jonah's dusty feet. He was cheerful and thorough in his duties. When a woman appeared on the ladder the child was quick to call to her.

"Mama, we have a stranger for supper."

Jonah smiled at his honest words, allowing the boy to wash his feet while he sat upon a rough stool.

The mother came quickly. "We thank you for this blessing. Our supper will be ready soon. Dan, run take care of his donkey and inform your father we have a guest."

Later, on the upper floor of the home, while the mother cleared his plate from the meal, Jonah sat back opposite the father and smiled.

"Have you traveled far?" the father asked.

"No. I have come from Gath-hepher and am going to Joppa. But there I intend to find a ship of Tarshish and travel as far as the sea will carry me."

The younger man's brow furrowed. "You hope to find

something?"

Jonah chuckled. "I do not go to find something." Then his face became serious. "I go from fear that the Lord intends me to travel to . . ." He stopped short, afraid he'd said too much, then mumbled, "To someplace else."

The man looked at Jonah curiously but remained silent.

Jonah decided it was unfair to burden the man with the reason for his travels. If he knew, he might feel greatly honored to offer his home to a prophet, but he might also feel it was a sin to shelter one who ran from God. Suddenly, Jonah wished he had not stopped at this good family's door.

To ease the tension, he asked if he might tell the children a story. The faces in the corners of the room brightened, and soon three children were gathered around his knees. A memory of sitting at the feet of Elijah flashed through Jonah's mind, and he chose one of the stories he had learned from the great prophet. Jonah leaned toward the children, looking into their deep, dark eyes, and began, "Joseph sat on the stone floor of the damp, dark prison. He was hungry and cold and he shivered, wishing he still had his coat his brothers had torn from him. He hadn't had any food all day, and the water tasted bad. Then he heard the footsteps of the prison guard coming toward his cell . . ."

That night, Jonah slept on a soft mat with a warm blanket over his shoulders and the glow from the fire's embers taking the chill from the early spring air. He was reminded of many such nights long ago when he had traveled with Elisha and found a place to stay in any home that offered them hospitality. Now Elisha was gone. Jonah missed the advice of the senior prophet—it would have been greatly appreciated now. But then Jonah thought of how Elisha had never shrunk from doing what the Lord called him to do. "But he wasn't called to go to Nineveh and perhaps put our own people in jeopardy!" He nearly said it aloud.

It was the evening of the fourth day when Jonah arrived, footsore and thirsty, at the city of Joppa. His donkey had become lame shortly out of Dor, so he had left him at a farm along the way. Jonah was past seventy years now, and though he was still very strong, the last stretch of the journey had caused his joints to ache.

Joppa, whose name meant *beautiful*, was built on a rounded hill over one hundred feet high. This hill gave the city a commanding view of the countryside and stretched gently down to the Great Sea to the west. To the north of the city lay the fertile Plain of Sharon, which stretched to Mount Carmel behind Jonah. To the southeast were flat, sandy dunes that slowly gave way to more fertile ground as the road from Jerusalem approached the city.

Coming from the north, Jonah plodded along up the well-traveled way, watching for a place to lay his bedroll for the night. He had decided not to ask for hospitality, since his stay might bring mixed blessings to a family. In addition, since Joppa was a Philistine city, Jonah wasn't sure he would be blessed as he had been in Dor to find a home friendly toward an Israelite.

As Jonah began ascending the hill to the city, he passed by olive groves and vineyards. On the western side of the hill, the sun was setting beyond the sea-filled horizon, causing the city to blaze with a golden light. On the eastern side of the hill, the shadows of the city lengthened and deepened into darkness. But the northern side where Jonah approached was caught in that ambiguous place between light and dark. Jonah turned off the road to his left, found a clearing in a secluded spot among the trees, and rolled out his bed. Beyond the reach of the cool sea breezes and with nothing to quench his thirst, he spent a restless, hot night attacked by flying insects.

As the sun rose over the bluish hills far to the east the next morning, Jonah woke to the first stirrings of people entering Joppa. He quickly rolled up his bed and joined the first of the country people who were clearly on their way to set up their stalls in a marketplace. Seeing a man with a cart of fresh milk and cheese, Jonah quickly hailed him.

"Peace to you, sir," Jonah called in a Canaanite dialect understood by most Philistines, Israelites, and Phoenicians. Although he was fluent in it, the communication between the various peoples was sketchy. Many Philistines still clung to their own tongue that was as foreign to the land as the Sea People who most influenced it. When the man did not acknowledge Jonah, he tried again, "Will you not sell milk to a weary traveler before you enter the marketplace?" The man did not slow his pace, but protested that it would not be convenient. Then Jonah offered to help him pull his cart the rest of the way to the city, and the man hesitated. Finally he nodded once, and Jonah gave him some copper in exchange for some fresh milk. Then, lifting the bar, the two men of different cultures and faiths pulled the cart up the hill and toward the gate of Joppa.

At the crest of the hill, Jonah stopped to gaze at the city as it spread down the western side below. Its buildings appeared in danger of toppling down to the sandy shore of the Great Sea, which was rimmed with rock outcroppings that gave the coastline a scalloped appearance. In the bay a few ships were anchored, tossing in the gentle swell of the tide. "Ah, the port to which the king of Tyre sent his cedars of Lebanon that Solomon used for the building of the temple in Jerusalem," Jonah observed. "It is good to see it again."

"You are not of these parts?" his companion asked.

"No, and it has been many years since I had cause to come here." Jonah sighed.

"Perhaps some things have changed, but perhaps not as many as have not changed. The Philistines are not easy taskmasters in the city, but the Phoenician traders from the Great Sea gain strength every year. To me it is the same. One greedy set of masters bends to another one. Yet each day I milk my goats, load my cart, and come to sell milk and cheese in the market, just as my father did and as my sons will. And the generations will pass."

The man leaned into the bar, and the wheels of his cart turned slowly forward, creaking under the burden they supported.

At the gate to the city, they waited in the growing line of merchants who had come to sell their wares. Jonah observed that the ones who passed by the quickest were placing several coins into the hands of the guards. As they got closer, his companion reached into the leather purse that hung inside his tunic.

"Good day, Sharif, O noble man," the guard said with a smirk.

"A blessed morning to you," Sharif responded, handing the man the required copper coins. He bent to pick up the bar to pull the cart into the city, but the guard put his foot against the wheel.

"Do not be in a hurry, Sharif." The guard grinned. "The day is not yet begun, and you have not introduced me to your companion."

"My name is Yunus," Jonah replied, giving the Aramaic version of his name in an attempt to divert the man from any prejudice toward Israelites. Then he extended his hand with five copper coins in it as he had seen Sharif do.

The large guard accepted the coins and then looked into his palm and laughed. "This is your first time to our city, is it not?" he asked. "How do I know of your sincerity that you will respect our city and our ways?"

Jonah was about to correct him—to say this was not his first visit—but his companion interrupted him. "Forgive me," Sharif said, reaching into his own leather purse again. "Indeed, it is his first time this year. But since I am a poor man and haven't much, I would be honored if you would let me give you the gift of a rare brass coin from the far reaches of Tarshish."

Sharif pulled out a worn coin, then shook the purse upside down now to emphasize that it contained no more. Then he polished the coin on his sleeve and with great ceremony, though with the right degree of reluctance, handed it to the guard with a bow. "I would be honored if you accepted this gift in behalf of my friend."

The guard looked at the coin with a greedy glint in his eyes and stepped aside. As the two men walked through the gate, Jonah turned to Sharif and said, "Thank you, my friend."

"It is good to understand the intelligence of these Philistines," Sharif answered under his breath. "This is one reason they will fall and be replaced by others, such as the hordes from Babylonia. An ignorant people will enslave themselves with their own stupidity."

"You are a philosopher, my friend." Jonah smiled. "But now I must bid you farewell. I need to find a ship that can take me to Tarshish."

"In the marketplace is a man who sells goods from faraway lands. He knows the ships well. He sets up next to me, and we talk of things. People drink my milk and eat my cheese while they look at his wares and listen to the stories he learns from sailors. It is a good arrangement. I will ask him."

Jonah helped Sharif pull his cart through the twisting streets and alleys of Joppa. Houses, with their tan or pale pink walls, square windows, and flat roofs, were stacked on either side of their winding way to the market square. A cool breeze from the sea blew away the smells of the city, and the streets were clean from a recent rainfall. In the early morning light, Joppa was as beautiful as its name claimed. Jonah stopped when he saw the bustling market and quoted, "'These were thy merchants in all sorts of things, in blue clothes, and broidered work, and in chests of rich apparel, bound with cords, and made of cedar, among thy merchandise.'"

Sharif only glanced toward Jonah, then began setting up his cart in the shade of an arch that spanned one of the streets leading to the square. "Peace to you, Danawi," Sharif said, nodding to the man next to him, who had set up a stall with portable tables piled high with rugs, blue pottery, silks, and other exotic items. Above the tables hung beaded scarves, copper necklaces, and earrings containing semi-precious stones. The man grinned at Sharif as he continued setting up his display. "Peace to you. You are slow today, Sharif."

"Yes, the greedy guards did not want my new friend to enter without an additional fee."

Sharif carefully blocked the wheels of his cart with bricks he had carried inside it. Then he lifted a board from the side of the cart and laid it across the back end. Onto the board he placed a small linen bundle the size of a loaf of bread. Jonah watched as Sharif carefully unwrapped the light linen cloth to reveal a soft cheese, looked at it carefully, and again wrapped it in the moist cloth. Then Sharif pulled out a sharp knife and sat it next to the cheese. Beside the cheese he laid similar round bundles, stacked two and three high.

"Allow me again to be your customer," Jonah pleaded.

"Your cheese smells as good as your milk tasted. Perhaps you could cut me a couple of copper coins' worth?" Jonah reached beneath his tunic and pulled out his leather purse. "You understand I will not offer you rare brass coins."

Sharif laughed as he cut a thick wedge of cheese and handed it to Jonah. "Perhaps it *was* rare," he said. "I did not look too closely so that I would not be found in a deliberate falsehood."

"Then a deliberate falsehood is more serious than an ignorant one?" Jonah questioned. "But which does more damage? A person who is known to deliberately deceive is rarely believed. But an ignorant one who proclaims what he desires to be truth, especially in defense of lazy or selfish habits, is often given great credit, and the lie is spread."

"Now who is the philosopher?" Sharif laughed. "But what of the man who deliberately deceives and is believed by many? Is he not the most dangerous?"

"Yea, it is so," Jonah said. "But it does not justify ignorance when knowledge is readily available. Though the deliberate deceiver bears a great burden of sin, the man who remains ignorant from neglect is also at fault."

"You convince me. Tomorrow I will tell the guard I am uncertain of the value of his rare brass coin and offer to trade it for these eggs, whose freshness I am likewise uncertain of," Sharif laughed again, gesturing to a rough net full of brown eggs he had just received in trade for a jar of milk.

Jonah smiled, but then glanced impatiently toward Danawi. During their conversation, women with babes wrapped about their middles and jars balanced on their heads had arrived, and Sharif had been busy ladling out milk. If one wanted cheese, the merchant paused to unwrap the one beside the knife and cut some for her to taste. His eyes never left his customers', and when they would nod, he would cut off the amount they asked for before carefully rewrapping the cheese in the moist cloth. Sometimes the exchange was made for copper coins, but often he accepted dates, olive oil, or other produce. This he placed in a tightly woven basket inside the cart, covering the basket with another damp cloth before replacing the lid.

When the sun began to climb in the sky and the marketplace began to empty until the heat of midday passed, Sharif remarked, "I have not forgotten that you wish to sail to Tarshish. I will speak to Danawi at once."

The ships of Tarshish did sing of thee in thy market: and thou wast replenished, and made very glorious in the midst of the seas.

Ezekiel 27:25

Chapter Seven

෧෨෧෨෧෨෧෨෧෨෧෨෧෨෧෨෧

Jonah crossed the deck behind the captain of the ship with whom he had negotiated passage two days before. The vessel was known as a ship of Tarshish because it was a trade ship that traveled the Great Sea and brought goods and materials bound for Jerusalem into the Joppa harbor.

Ships of Tarshish were the largest seagoing vessels that sailed between the isles and ports of the sea. Because the shoreline of Joppa was rocky, these and other ships would anchor a mile out in the harbor, where they were tossed with the tides and winds of the open sea beyond. Smaller boats were in constant employ between the larger ships and the tradesmen on shore, bringing goods into Joppa in exchange for dates, olive oil, barley, wheat, corn, and other goods to be traded throughout the Assyrian Empire, Egypt, and the far reaches of the Great Sea.

Jonah had arrived on one of the smaller boats and carefully climbed up the knotted net the sailors used to board. He stood on the cypress-wood deck with his legs braced in a wide stance, pausing to accustom himself to the gentle rolling of the waves and looking around at the craftsmanship of the ship. It was a large ship with fifteen rowers on each side. In the ship's bow stood a single mast crafted from a tall cedar, clearly chosen for its strength and straightness.

The record of Ezra came to Jonah's mind: "They gave money also . . . to them of Tyre, to bring cedar trees from Lebanon to the sea of Joppa." The sail, made of white Egyptian canvas, was bound to the yard—the beam that stretched across the mast—but could be lowered in bad weather.

The stern of the ship rose above the water in an arch that curved back over the ship. Beneath it was a deep-colored canopy of blue that draped the sides and sheltered the captain, pilot, and steersman. A bowsprit, like a sharp horn, jutted out over the water at the bow, and above it stared a pair of painted eyes, piercing the distance with a discerning stare.

Lining both sides of the ship were cypress benches on which the rowers sat. The oars were carved from the oak of Bashan. Here the famed sea dogs of Sidon and Aradus would strain their muscles in moving the ship through the sea. The rowers were under the command of the chief steersman, or master, who would take his place beneath the canopy in the rear of the ship.

Five men sat on benches mending ropes as Jonah and the captain passed by. Jonah wrinkled his nose against the lingering stench of old sweat, but then a clean sea breeze blew past, and he breathed in deeply.

The captain gave Jonah to the care of a sailor and then turned back to speak to his pilot. Jonah followed the sailor below through a doorway in the deck.

"What brings you to our ship?" the man asked.

"I am running from my God." Jonah grimaced.

"Do we not all at some time?"

He led Jonah down to the cargo hold—beneath the beams, smells, and noises. Squeezed among the chests, amphora jars, and baskets hung rope-strung beds. The sailor indicated a bed that Jonah could use, and then he left.

Jonah put his pack into the foot of the suspended bed and looked around. The ship was fully laden and ready to sail. Into the rear were packed the most recent goods from Sidon, Tyre, and Joppa, filling the majority of the hull. Near the fore were remnants of goods obtained from other ports. From Egypt came bales of fine linen and cotton, some of it with elaborate and colorful embroidery. From Arabia came amphora jars of spices, with their pointed or rounded bottoms nestled firmly into boxes of sand. From them, like heat waves, came the smell of cassia, calamus, cinnamon, and frankincense—all combining to fill the air with heavy aromas.

The ship carried blue fabric, embroidered work, chests of rich apparel from Lebanon and upper Assyria, many varieties of pottery, metal utensils, gold and silver ornaments, mirrors, glass beads, and smelling bottles. It also held muslin from Hindustan, a few shawls from Kashmir, carpets from Babylonia, and pearls from the gulf below Ur. Jonah lifted the lid of a chest and found remnants of expensive papyrus from Egypt.

Finally, the ship carried remnants from perhaps another year, when it had made a trip to Iberia—chests of silver, iron, tin, and lead. This would have been the most valuable of the cargo. Absent was the coarser pottery and bronze vessels that could be manufactured in any city of the world.

At the beginning of the journey there might also have been wool and goat's hair bundles from Arabia, as well as cloth for chariots, wrought iron, gold, and precious stones. From India and Arabia there might have been ivory and ebony. But many of those goods had been traded along the way.

Though the ship was depleted of the wares of some countries, it was abundant in items from its recent stops at Tyre and Sidon—the cities of the Phoenicians. And it was now filling with the wares traded for in Joppa. The crew would be wealthy at the end of this voyage.

Jonah pondered the distances the ship had sailed and where this trip might lead. He thought about the soundness of the timbers; though strong and well fitted, they creaked with each swell of the sea as the boat gently rose and fell. Although he had sailed only a few times before, Jonah was grateful that the sea did not turn his stomach as it did the stomachs of many others not used to its endless rising and falling.

As he thought about the cedar mast above, words came to him from a song of King David: "The righteous shall flourish like the palm tree: he shall grow like a cedar in Lebanon." The words smote his heart. Rather than flourish, he was running from the Lord, the Holy One of Israel. Was he as a cedar about to be hewed down? Would he be able to flee to a place where the great arm of Jehovah did not reach?

*Wanderers are many on earth, and the greatest of these is
Man, who rides the ocean and takes his way through the deeps,
through wind-swept valleys of perilous seas that surge and sway.*

Sophocles, *Antigone*

Chapter Eight

〜〜〜〜〜〜〜〜〜〜〜〜〜〜

Having dispensed with his only paying passenger and having consulted the pilot, the captain gave orders that all men return to their posts. Immediately, the rowers filled the benches, and the steersman took his place at the oak helm and grasped the tiller, which controlled the great rudder beneath. A youthful and muscular sailor stood ready to assist the master if the winds became strong. The pilot went to his much-guarded charts under the canopy.

After a week in port, the sailors were clearly eager to be at sea again. There was an air of expectation and happiness among them. Obviously, it had been a profitable journey so far. The prevailing wind out of the west that had brought the ship so smoothly into the Joppa harbor blew softly, and the conditions were right for the ship to be rowed out to where it would catch the winds that would carry the crew southward toward Egypt and beyond—as far from Nineveh as Jonah could go.

The master began calling out orders, the great oars dipped

into the sea, and the ship began to move. In the early morning light, the ship's shadow kept pace as the vessel turned about until the rising sun was at the rowers' backs. It was an easy row to bring the ship out of the harbor. Then the captain shouted for the sail to be unfurled. Obedient sailors tugged at two ropes that held the bundled fabric snugly to the yard. A large white cloth, with an embroidered design in blue, green, and gold, billowed down like a sheet being shaken in the wind. Other sailors held tightly to ropes affixed to the lower corners of the sail. They adjusted the angle of the sail according to the captain's orders and then fastened the ropes tightly to large iron bolts. The westerly wind snatched the sail, whipped it taut, and carried the ship forward with a lunge. By then, the rowers had already laid their oars to rest in the oarlocks until further order.

A few of the sailors said a quick prayer to Astarte, the "lady of the sea" and goddess of the earth, for a profitable voyage and a safe return to their wives and children before winter. Others looked over their shoulders toward the dwarf image of a Cabeiri pair carved into the prow of the ship beneath the bowsprit. The image assured them that the ship had been placed under the protection of the Cabeiri, and that their vessel would be preserved.

The pilot gave directions to the captain, who navigated the ship through the blue waters toward Gaza. From there they would continue, traveling parallel to the Way of the Sea until they reached the Egyptian port of Djane, or Zoan, as Jonah's people called it.

They sailed peacefully for most of the day and looked to reach Gaza by night. Gaza was not a major trading port like Tyre and Joppa but merely a place to dock that night; they would continue their journey the next day.

For supper Jonah was given fresh dates, cheese, and barley

bread served with olive oil. He thanked the men and then carried his meal below. He ate in the hold, wanting to be out of the way and to say his prayers in private. Though it was still light above, the hold was dark. Jonah said his prayers, directing them toward the temple at Jerusalem. He prayed from habit, but as he crawled into his rope-strung bed, a now-familiar echo rang through his head: "Go to Nineveh, that great city, and cry against it."

Jonah cringed in his heart. He had convinced himself that his running away was a heroic act. By refusing to be the prophet that helped convince Nineveh's people to repent, he would spare his own people from destruction by the Assyrians. Now he wondered if, in truth, he was refusing to take the word of God to Nineveh because the Assyrians were his despised enemy. And perhaps fear was part of it, for Jonah knew that in Assyria, enemies were flayed alive or made to endure other such tortures.

"Such a wicked people are not worthy of God's forgiveness," he declared aloud to the darkness. But guilt at disobeying the voice of God troubled him as he fell asleep, and terrible images of Nineveh gyrated through his dreams.

They were an hour from Gaza when the sky began to darken quickly as storm clouds closed in. The growing wind filled the sail, and the sea became violent. The captain promptly ordered the sail and yard lowered to the deck and the rowers to take the ship to shore. While the pilot scoured his charts to find a safe place to land, the master at the stern earnestly began a chant in union with the rhythm of the goat-skinned drum he beat with the palms of his hands. The cadence directed the strokes of the oars and brought the ship under the control of the oarsmen. But the master's voice dwindled in the howling wind as the tempest of the sea crashed upon the ship with increasing force.

As the wind and sea pounded the ship, some of the sailors cried that the vessel would be broken; others fell to their knees, praying to the god of their choice. Great waves heaved over the ship's sides, drenching the sailors and knocking them about. The oarsmen clung to their oars as much for safety as to propel the ship to shore. Leaning into them with all their strength, they battled but could not overpower the sea. The tempest was such a one as is rarely seen, but is later spoken of in hushed tones by a warm fire under a sturdy roof. Few had survived to tell firsthand the tale of such a tempest as this one.

The sailors, who had been bailing water, could no longer keep up with the deluge. It poured over the deck and past the hatch that led to the hold. There it ran down through the spaces in search of a drain. Before long, the men could barely strain against the increasing weight from the water rising in the hold. "We must lighten the load or we will perish!" the pilot cried to the captain. The captain peered through the darkness but could see no land beyond the mountains of waves. He stared at the deep purple walls crashing around him, then looked to the faces of the sailors and oarsmen about him. They were men straining with their last measure of strength, men who had sailed with him through other storms and battles with pirates, men whom he prized above the goods in his hold or even his ship itself. He nodded once but said nothing.

Immediately the order was given and the sailors began to throw water barrels and other heavy objects overboard. Opening the hatch, they poured down into the hold and began passing the precious cargo from one to another, carrying it into the driving rain above and dumping it into the cold, black, roiling water.

When the wind first began to howl and the sea began to toss violently, Jonah wakened with a start and then cowered in fear in his bed as the storm continued to gain force. His only and repeated thought was, *What have I done?*

He looked toward the open hatch as stooped, spectral figures began descending into the hold. He watched them grab the first amphora jar and pass it up through the opening. Jonah lay still, afraid the sailors would remember him, perceive the guilt upon his face, and lay the storm to his blame.

The men worked soundlessly and with grim expressions. The cargo they were dumping represented their pay for long months away from home, but they knew that only when the ship itself was in danger would the captain consider such a measure.

When all had been cast into the hungry sea, the sailors stood momentarily watching the storm continue to beat on them. What more could they do to survive this night? The murmuring of the men reached the master at the tiller, and he called to the captain. The captain made his way carefully across the pitching deck and past the oarsmen, who were straining with tired muscles to save them all. He stood before the steersman and listened. Then, without another word, he nodded, and the master gave the tiller to the strength of his apprentice, rose, and stumbled toward the hatch.

Soon, down in the wet and now-empty hold, the shipmaster stood in water up to his knees. Placing his hands on Jonah's shoulders, he shook the old man and shouted above the din, "What meanest thou, O sleeper? Arise!"

The Phoenician language was similar to Hebrew, so Jonah had been able to communicate with the men of the ship, though imperfectly. When the master shouted at him, Jonah sat up, startled at his sharpness. The master reached out and steadied Jonah before he tumbled from his bed. Jonah barely recognized the wet, bearded man before him.

The sailor spoke again. "We are in peril! The ship at this moment is near to breaking. Each man has prayed to his god but to no account. Arise. Call upon thy god, if it so be that thy god will think upon us, that we perish not."

Jonah tumbled from bed, feeling the cold bite of the water on his bare feet. He followed the man, and they emerged into the vortex above them. The crew, huddled against the elements, clung to the mast and to whatever else was firmly affixed on deck.

"Sir, may I speak?" the pilot shouted to the captain, who nodded. "Sir, the men have conferred and have decided that the fury of a god is being vent upon us because of the disobedience of one of us. Because no one has come forward, they have determined to cast lots to know for whose cause this evil is upon us, that we perish not. With your permission, sir . . ."

The captain merely nodded and stumbled to where the canopy had once hung. At his feet, chained to the deck, was the jar that held the charts that were prized more than the wares thrown into the sea. The jar's lid was tightly fitted and tied down with a strong cord.

He stood in silence, braced against the tossing deck, his back to the men.

A sailor held out a handful of stones that he carried in his pocket. Others brought forth similar smooth rocks, used for games of chance, as well as casting lots. Finally there were enough stones to represent each man on the ship. On each stone was a drawing of an animal or a symbol of a god. Each man chose a stone and then returned it to the pilot, who stepped forward and tossed them all against one of the horizontal boards that rose like a short rail or wall around the ship. The men then gathered and looked hard in the darkness to see whose stone had landed closest to the wooden side. The stones had fallen in random order, scattered by the wind and the tossing of the ship, but one stone had landed right up against the edge and was unmoved. Slowly the pilot reached for it and then held his palm open to show a stone with the symbol of a fish. "Whose stone is this?"

"It is mine," Jonah said. He grew pale and immediately felt ill. More than the storm was tossing his stomach.

"Tell us, we pray thee," the pilot said as each man looked to Jonah, "for whose cause is this evil upon us? What is thy occupation? And whence comest thou? What is thy country? And of what people art thou?"

"I am a Hebrew," Jonah said, sparking a look of confusion on the faces of the men about him. "I fear the Lord, the God of heaven, which hath made the sea and the dry land."

The sailor who had escorted him below asked, "Is it not so that you said you flee from your god? Why hast thou done this?"

The sailors gasped, and fear crossed their faces as Jonah hung his head.

In agony, the pilot asked, "What shall we do unto thee, that the sea may be calm unto us?"

Jonah looked around him at the raging tempest. He remembered the rising water below, and he thought of the cherished cargo that had been sacrificed. He looked to the angry waters that beat over the edge of the ship. What had he done indeed? Had he thought that the Lord God who had created the earth would not follow him beyond Israel?

Jonah turned to the men and replied, "Take me up, and cast me forth into the sea; so shall the sea be calm unto you; for I know that for my sake this great tempest is upon you."

The fear on the men's faces turned to horror, and they

looked away from Jonah. The master of the oars spoke for the first time: "Before we consider this desperate course, we will row again to bring the ship to land—not just the oarsmen but every man on the ship!"

In obedience, the men, who had no strength left, called upon their will and bent their backs again to the oars. The master beat out the strokes against the wind, and even the pilot took his place on the bench beside a large man from Sidon. Jonah watched in the driving rain as they pulled, raised the oars, pushed them, and pulled again. Again and again they pulled and pushed. The timbers of the ship creaked and the mast swayed, ready to snap. A man in the fourth bench from the stern on the port side suddenly collapsed. Still the cadence rang out and still the men pulled against the waves and the wind. But their efforts proved futile. Two more men soon collapsed, and the master of oars at the tiller hesitated.

Jonah stepped forward. "Enough." His voice was weak, and it was felt rather than heard over the roar of the wind and waves. The drumbeat signaled a stop.

"It is time," Jonah declared. "Do not wait longer, for the storm does not abate, and I will not have you perish for my sake."

He went to the side of the ship and hung on, looking toward the men. Slowly they gathered around. They were about to pick Jonah up when the captain stepped into their midst and placed a hand on the man about to lift Jonah's legs. He raised his eyes to the sky, addressing the heavens rather than the men: "We beseech thee, O Lord, who is Jonah's God, to not let us perish for this man's life, and lay not upon us innocent blood. For thou, O Lord, hast done as it pleased thee."

The captain looked to his men and nodded. They then took up Jonah and cast him into the sea. As he fell to the water below, he felt the covering on his head snatched away and carried beyond sight in the dark, driving rain. He had the fleeting thought that without his head covered he was unworthy to call upon the Lord. Then he hit the surface of the sea with a stunning blow. The waves quickly closed around him, and he sank into the depths.

Above, the men on the ship leaned against the side, straining for a sight of him. Then as if a hand had passed before a candle, the wind ceased, the seas calmed, and the clouds blew away like wisps of smoke.

The sun was just setting, but the half-light at the ending of the day seemed like noon after the darkness of the tempest. The sailors surveyed the damage around them. Oars and sailors lay broken and battered, and tangled ropes littered the deck. But the sail was still bound to the yard, and the mast still stood. Fish, heaved up by the waves, flopped about on the deck. The exhausted men chose ten large fish and cast the remainder into the sea. They placed these ten in an amphora jar that they filled with seawater. The pilot looked long at the land a dim mile away and announced that they were still within sailing distance of Gaza for the night.

Later that night on the shores of Gaza, the men gathered around the captain at the edge of a large fire. Onto the blaze they tossed the ten fish as an offering to Jonah's God, whom he had named "the Lord." Each man prayed that he would not offend the Creator of earth and sea.

Out in that sea, Jonah had surfaced once and filled his lungs with air. He had looked wide-eyed at the billowing surge around him and would have wept but for the shadow that soon rose before him. It came up out of the sea and gaped open a black cavern before him. Then Jonah had felt himself falling with a great rush of water into the cavern. All turned black . . . and silent.

The ribs and terrors in the whale,
Arched over me a dismal gloom,
While all God's sun-lit waves rolled by,
And lift me deepening down to doom.
I saw the opening maw of hell,
With endless pains and sorrows there;
Which none but they that feel can tell.

Herman Melville, *Moby Dick*

Chapter Nine

∽∾∽∾∽∾∽∾∽∾∽∾∽∾∽

After a great rushing, scraping against sharp teeth, then a squeezing, pushing sensation, Jonah lost consciousness. When he began to sense his body again, he was in total darkness. Slime and weeds were wrapped about his head, and he shut his eyes tightly. The stench was overwhelming, but Jonah found that his arms were pinned against his sides so he could do nothing to cover his nose and mouth. Each breath brought in the smell of half-digested fish, the tendrils of weeds, and very little air. Having determined that he was within the belly of a great fish, he began to black out again, giving himself up for dead. After a few hours, he revived only to find he was still in a mortal hell.

For three days and three nights, Jonah lay in the belly of the fish, unable to move, barely able to breathe, with weeds wrapped about his head. Wryly, he thought to himself, *The Lord has provided a covering for my head.* He was unaware of how much time passed; he only knew he was becoming increasingly thirsty. Yet he did not die. Why would the Lord allow a fish to save him only so he could die slowly? Was it so he could come to recognize the futility of his actions? Finally, in the darkness and stench, in and out of consciousness, he recognized that he should never have tried to run from God.

There, helpless beyond the aid of man, humbled and ashamed, he cried "out of the belly of hell" unto the Lord: "For thou hadst cast me into the deep, in the midst of the seas; and the floods compassed me about: all thy billows and thy waves passed over me." He paused, realizing he had been praying silently. With renewed determination he began to voice his prayer through a raspy throat, dry from lack of water. "I am cast out of thy sight; yet I will look again toward thy holy temple. The waters compassed me about, even to the soul: the depth closed me round about, the weeds were wrapped about my head."

Suddenly, there was a great movement and his stomach lurched to his throat. The fish that held him went into a dive, and Jonah was slammed forward, jamming his head against ribs. Then the fish rolled and began to climb. Jonah slid backward, and his bare feet plunged into slime and pieces of smaller fish. He prayed fervently: "I went down to the bottoms of the mountains; the earth with her bars was about me forever: yet hast thou brought up my life from corruption, O Lord my God." Yet there was no peace within his bony prison and again the fish dived, this time with a roll that sent a liquid mass into Jonah's mouth. Then mercifully, darkness again closed around his panicked mind.

The fish was calm when Jonah revived again. He spat the weeds and unknown muddy substance from his mouth, then curled and flexed his fingers and toes in assessment. Still terrified because his circumstances remained unchanged, he cried out, "Why am I left here to perish slowly?" There was no answer—just the cold, wet, bony bed and terrible stench. Finally, he began to calm his mind and to reason. Perhaps it was not the Lord's will that he die in the fish. This time he prayed, "What is required of me?" Then, just as the sailors had offered burnt offerings to the Lord, Jonah also felt a desire to appease his God with a sacrifice. But from the belly of a fish he had nothing to offer, so he called out from his heart, "I will sacrifice unto thee with the voice of thanksgiving." And so, through the remainder of the dark, nauseous, and cramped three days, Jonah prayed to the Lord, who heard and calmed Jonah's heart.

For three days, the fish swam north—past Joppa, past the great port of Tyre, to the ancient port of Sidon. There the great fish entered the bay. And when the Lord commanded, the fish vomited Jonah upon the dry land.

*Trust in the Lord with all thine heart; and lean
not unto thine own understanding.*

Proverbs 3:5

Chapter Ten

⫷⫷⫷⫷⫷⫷⫷⫷⫷⫷⫷⫷⫷⫷⫷⫷

Jonah lay in the sand for some time before the warm sun, mounting ever higher in the morning sky, penetrated his stupor. He stirred enough to realize that the salty, fishy taste in his mouth had been replaced by the earthy taste of sand, and that the cold of the sea had been replaced by the heat of the sun. Instead of darkness and a terrible stink, he sensed a golden light and a warm breeze. Smelling grass and baked earth, he took a deep breath and gladly filled his lungs. With his face still in the sand, Jonah began to utter a prayer of gratitude that he had been spared.

And the word of the Lord came unto Jonah the second time, saying, "Arise, go unto Nineveh, that great city, and preach unto it the preaching that I bid thee."

Jonah responded, "Thy will is mine. Forgive me for my lack of obedience and faith."

With new determination, Jonah pushed himself up and looked around. Above him, on a crest of the sand, a man stood, staring down at Jonah. When the man saw Jonah look at him, he suddenly turned and ran.

"Wait," Jonah called in Aramaic. His voice came out raspy and faint. Aramaic was the language of the Aramaeans and close to the Hebrew language. Jonah had learned it so he could read accounts written in that language. Still, reading and speaking were two different things, and either way, there was no response. In fact, the man was no longer in sight beyond the ridge above the shore.

Jonah sat where he was, with his back to the sandy ridge and his face toward the sea. In the harbor were a Phoenician ship and several small fishing vessels. Fishermen were unloading their catch from the night before and sorting fish on the beach. Their vessels bobbed and tugged in the sea, while securely tied to shore. The men were a stocky, grizzled bunch, but they were too far off for Jonah to hear their talk or for them to hear him if he called. He sat there gathering his strength and watching the fishermen at work.

The seaport city brought back vague memories of his early years in Zarephath. Often, as a boy, he would go down to the sea to watch the sailors bring in their catch. However, the village of his childhood had not had a port like this one, so there had been no merchant vessels like the one that bobbed in the wake below.

Finally, Jonah realized what the seamen were doing, sorting through nets that had been pulled from shallow, tidal pools. The nets were filled with small shells that the men pried open. Inside were the murex snails from whose glands the famous purple dye was extracted. The dye was so rare that the purple cloth they sold around the Great Sea was bought only by the wealthy and, therefore, was known as the color of royalty. But even from a distance, the smell of fish and the sea became too much for the man who had spent three days and three nights in the belly of a fish. At last Jonah arose and turned himself toward the town, walking inland away from the sea and toward Nineveh and the Assyrian Empire.

The path he followed twisted and turned and joined other paths. It passed by dwelling places that began as single houses divided by gardens, and soon began to group then merge into the main city. Jonah soon became lost on the maze of streets that wound around and between houses that had windows atop of windows. The houses were narrow and squeezed together, yet they were taller than the houses of Joppa. He strained his neck, looking up at the triple-layered buildings.

When a man brushed by him, Jonah asked in his best Aramaic, "Excuse me sir, what city is this?" The man backed away from Jonah and looked at him as if he were a mad man, then turned and hurried away. Jonah looked down at his clothes, which were covered with greenish black mud. They clung to him, torn and twisted. His hands were similarly colored, and he realized that his beard and face must have borne the same covering.

He walked on, turning corners, looking for a place to clean himself and get a drink. People moved away from him, yet stared after him as he passed. Nobody would talk to him when he asked where he might find water. Finally, he found a plaza with a well in the center.

When he approached, people backed away, mothers grabbed their children, and a young boy lobbed a small stone at him. "Go away," he called, "this is not a beggar's well."

"I am not a beggar," Jonah said. "I was cast into the sea from a ship during a storm."

"There has been no storm here for three days," a woman stated.

"I have been traveling in the belly of a fish for these three days." Jonah almost whispered, due to his dry throat and out of fear of the scoffing that was sure to follow.

But then a woman spoke plainly for all to hear: "My husband said he saw a man thrown on the beach this morning from the mouth of a large fish." A gasp went up among the people. Sheepishly she added, "I told him not to drink so much wine."

The people stopped, and a look of wonder passed over many faces.

"I was with him," said a man who stepped through the gathering crowd. Jonah recognized him as the man that had stood above him but ran when he called. "It is true. I also saw the fish spew a man up onto the beach. I stayed and saw that it was this man, but then I ran when he revived. We thought he was a god from the sea."

"I am no god," Jonah said. "But my God has sent me on a journey. I did not know how long I was in the sea until now. I do not even know what city this is. If I may drink from your well and wash myself, I will be gone. I am going to Nineveh."

The people moved away from the well, allowing Jonah to approach. Some had puzzled expressions on their faces. Some knelt down, even though Jonah had told them he was just a man. If he was a god from the sea, they did not wish to offend him. But a bold, young man spoke near his elbow as Jonah splashed water onto his face: "You are in Sidon," he stated.

Jonah stopped and looked toward the sea. "I had wondered as much," he said to himself. "My home as a child is so close . . ." Then he realized that the fish had brought him north, back toward the road to Nineveh. All his excuses and fabricated good intentions had not stopped the work of the Lord. Not only had he been saved from his own foolishness, but he had been set firmly back onto the path he had been called to follow.

"Why are you going to Nineveh?" It was the same voice that had told him where he was.

Jonah looked down to see a thin-faced lad who looked about twelve or thirteen years old. "I am going," he paused, "because my God has sent me there."

"You are not a god?"

"No, but I serve my God."

Jonah began to wash himself, thinking that the boy would leave him now.

"Which God is sending you to Nineveh? Is it Sin, the god of Sidon?" the persistent boy continued.

"No, I serve the great Jehovah, Maker of heaven and earth and all things thereon. He is the God of Abraham, Isaac, and Jacob—the God who divided the Red Sea for Moses so that the children of Israel might pass over, and who closed it again so the Egyptians would be destroyed."

The boy pondered and then responded, "I don't know that story. I would like to hear it sometime and about this Abraham and the others. I will help you with your pronunciation, though."

Exhausted, Jonah looked at the boy and wondered how he could politely excuse himself.

The lad then added, "I can also help you get to Nineveh. I can help you find a caravan and a mule."

Then Jonah thought he understood. The boy was looking for an employer. "I cannot pay you," Jonah said. "And I do not have means to purchase a mule. My purse was lost in the Great Sea."

The boy's face fell and he turned to leave. Then suddenly

he returned. "Has your God really sent you to Nineveh?" he asked. Jonah nodded. "My father can always use a camel master. I will talk to him."

"But I know nothing of camels." Jonah sighed.

"Do you have anything you can offer?" the boy asked, beginning to sound like doubtful.

Jonah thought back to his youth, when his grandfather had charged him with herding his many goats—a task Jonah had done for five years. "I can herd goats," he said, smiling weakly.

"That is boy's work," the boy said. Then he looked again at Jonah, who by now had washed himself and had taken a long drink from the clean, cool water. Jonah's eyes were deep like a night sky and yet troubled like a summer storm. His beard and the hair that wrapped around his head from one ear to the other was stark white (though Jonah did not know this change had occurred), and his balding head was pale pink, as though it was never exposed to the sun. The boy's eyes widened, and Jonah wondered if the Lord had urged him to help this poor prophet.

"I will ask my father if he needs a goat herder," the boy suggested. "My father has come to Sidon to trade for purple cloth. Tomorrow we cross the hills to meet the main caravan at Damascus. Perhaps you can be useful until then." He paused then tipped his head sideways, examining Jonah more closely. Then he asked, "Why did your God not provide you with the means to get to Nineveh?"

Jonah smiled. "It seems he has."

The boy turned and started down one of the five streets that led from the plaza. He was nearly out of sight when he turned. "Are you not coming?"

Jonah hurried over to where the boy waited.

"My name is Darius," the boy said as Jonah fell into step

beside him. "It looks as though you need a covering for your head."

Jonah laughed. "Yes, Darius, I do. And my name is Jonah."

Heav'n forming each on other to depend,
A master, or a servant, or a friend,
Bids each on other for assistance call,
'Till one man's weakness grows the strength of all.

Alexander Pope, *Essay on Man*

Chapter Eleven

〰〰〰〰〰〰〰〰〰〰〰〰

*J*onah barely lifted the pole that rested on his right shoulder. He lifted the pad he had fashioned from an old rag and transferred it to his left shoulder with his left hand, while his right had steadied the pole. Then he ducked under the pole, switching the weight to the left side. The man he followed that carried the other end glanced back with an angry look, but proceeded up the steep, narrow path through the hills without slowing his pace. From the pole hung five bundles of purple cloth that Darius' father had traded for in Sidon. There were three such pairs of men carrying the precious cargo that would be transferred to camels when they joined the caravan in Damascus. The cloth would be highly prized in Nineveh, far to the east. Jonah endeavored to keep up with the younger, stronger legs of the other porters, but there was no denying he was at least forty years older. Darius had insisted on using the old man, and Jonah feared that Darius' father would soon discover his weakness.

South of Sidon were the seaports of Tyre, Akko, and then Dor. From Dor the caravan route that followed the Way of the Sea turned inland in a northeastern direction. It passed through Hazor and then continued northeast to Damascus, eliminating the need to cross the hills to the north that separated Sidon and Tyre from the inland route. Because Darius' father had left the caravan at Dor, he'd had to travel quickly to arrive in Sidon, bargain for his purchases, and leave in time to cross the hills and arrive at Damascus when the caravan did. Since he rode a mule, as did Darius, the porters who walked had to maintain a steady pace with few stops for rest.

The heavy wooden pole began to cut into Jonah's left shoulder. He looked at the broad backs of the other porters ahead of him and glanced back at the two behind. They had brown faces with the deep creases that came from hard labor in the sun. Jonah began to concentrate on small goals. *First, make it to that boulder where the path turns.* At the boulder, the goal became to go as far as an ancient tree that had a twisted trunk. At the tree, he allowed himself to change the pole to a different shoulder, gaining a bit of strength to be able to set a new visual goal. When Jonah became too tired to lift his head, needing to conserve even that energy for the slow, steady climb, he began to count. *One hundred more steps, then I can change the pole again,* he promised himself. Soon even the effort to lift the pole became excruciating.

If Jonah had gone directly to Nineveh and not to Joppa, then through the belly of a fish, he would have still have had his purse. He could have purchased a mule and joined a caravan much sooner. He sighed, knowing his agony was not a punishment but rather a natural consequence.

They climbed all day, taking a short rest in the morning and an extended one, when the day was hottest, for a cold meal.

As the day progressed and the sun lowered in the sky, the hills around them blocked the light and the path became harder to see. Finally, the guide stopped in an open area before the next assent. Jonah set down his burden where directed, then stumbled to a large boulder to sit.

His legs ached, his feet had blisters, and his shoulders felt like they were on fire. Darius was not to be seen because he and his father had ridden over the ridge to scout out the morning's trail. Soon Jonah was put to work helping set up camp and preparing a simple stew from dried meat and a few root vegetables. When two tents were erected, Jonah was given the task of tending the stew while the stronger men cut logs and carried water from a nearby stream.

Supper was eaten in silence because everyone was exhausted. Jonah was chewing some stew-soaked flatbread when Darius approached him.

"Where do you come from?" the boy asked.

"Gath-hepher."

"Oh. I was hoping you came from Jerusalem."

"No, I am an Israelite," Jonah explained. "Jerusalem is in Judah. But I have been there many times. In fact, my wife is on her way there right now to offer sacrifices at the temple."

"What kind of sacrifices?" Darius' eyes were large.

"Only animals. Goats, lambs, doves, occasionally a large ram or ox." Jonah knew the boy had thought of the wicked sacrifices offered to pagan deities and that this answer would seem dull.

"Is it true that Hebrew babies are taught to chant their prayers before they can walk, and to read before they can run?"

Jonah smiled as the memory of a similar conversation with his granddaughter Adira came to mind. "Hebrew children are taught to value the writings of the prophets.. But they learn at the same rate as other children."

"Perhaps," Darius began, "but not many children are taught to read. Were you taught to read?"

"Yes," Jonah answered slowly, realizing that something he had taken for granted could be a novelty here in the wilderness. "Have you had a teacher of reading?"

"No. I am learning about trade and caravans. Why do I need to read?"

Jonah stopped, unsure of how to answer. He treasured the scrolls in his home. When he had left, he had entrusted their care to his oldest son with the understanding that he could borrow them anytime. If he returned.

"I promised to tell you the story of Abraham," Jonah said at last. "Sit down." Darius did and Jonah began, "The cords that bound Abraham to the golden altar were strong. He strained at them, but they only tightened. The priest stood poised with his knife raised, the reflection of the fire flashed on the blade. So Abraham began to pray . . ."

After supper everyone retired to their beds, Darius with his father, and Jonah to the larger tent with the porters and guide. He was in terrible pain because his muscles had tightened as they sat around the fire. He lay on his bedroll stiffly, both arms straight at his sides, and longed for the rescue of sleep. The glow from the fire danced on the tent wall, a solitary snake moved onto a rock near the fire for warmth, and Jonah finally received relief from his agony, falling asleep even before the porters had begun to breathe in steady counterpoint.

In Sidon the sky still glowed with the setting sun reflecting on the waters of the sea. In the shadows between buildings and beneath overhanging balconies, a man paused in a plaza around a fountain as if waiting. He was prematurely bent from his work of hauling fishing nets, and his hands were stained a permanent purple that looked black in the increasing darkness. That very day his wife had told him they were expecting another child. That would make five, and he barely provided for them now. She had been tight-lipped because he had stopped to drink wine with others from work before going home. Her coldness and her news had angered him, and once again he'd thought of the conversation of his drinking companions.

It had begun about the man who had come from the sea and how two witnesses had sworn a large fish had vomited him onto the shore. They discussed whether or not he was a god, despite his denial of being one. Someone knew the man from the sea wanted to travel to Nineveh, that his god had told him to go there. Then another man had mentioned the trader who had bought a great quantity of purple cloth that would sell well in Harran, Nineveh, and beyond. He had known that the trader traveled with his son and he'd heard they were hiring porters to travel as far as Damascus. "Maybe the sea god could hire as a porter," someone had suggested. At this the group had laughed in derision, since gods did not need to hire out for menial labor. Neither would the messenger of a god. The men had begun to break off then and go to their homes to discuss the news of the marketplace with their wives over suppers of greasy fish and onions.

Two men had stayed behind, the man with the bent back and purple hands, and a taller man who had been a craftsman with glass until a few months previously. No one knew why the glass craftsman was no longer employed in his trade, or why he had seemed to prosper more since. No one wanted to know. But tonight he whispered a suggestion of a plan, and when it was met with curiosity, he had expanded his idea. Finally, he said simply, "I'll be at the fish fountain at dusk if you want to come."

So the stooped man waited in the increasing darkness, and then as the sun slid its final descent of the night into the sea, two shadows separated from the darkness of the city plaza and approached the man who had waited. Few words were exchanged, but five men in all had left Sidon and followed the trail the mules and porters had taken that morning.

They traveled light and the full moon lit the trail. Still, they did not have a guide, so when the trail became faint or divided, they often became confused. None of them were skilled enough to discern the clear signs of the group that had preceded them, so by the time they arrived at the camp, the diffused light before dawn was filling the sky in a soft pink.

The tall craftsman had become the silently acknowledged leader, and he began to direct the men who huddled with him in the brush. There were two tents: one for Darius, his father, and the bundles of cloth; and one for the porters and guide. A man was sent to listen and returned with the information of which tent contained the snoring of many men. It was closest to the trail with the door facing east toward where the dinner had been cooked. The other tent was beyond with its back to a rock wall. The men were divided, two to stand ready at the first tent's entrance, and three to obtain the bundles from the tent to the rear.

The bent man weighed the knife he held in his left hand. It was the one he used to open murex shells so the dye could be extracted. He shifted it to his right hand, then back to his left, following the two men before him through the fading darkness of the camp.

Jonah had been dreaming about his journey in the belly of the large fish, but this time he was about to be crunched by the addition of another passenger that the fish had swallowed. He awoke with a start, but then as the snoring and smells around him reminded him of where he was he rolled over with the intent of returning to sleep. A cracked branch and a stifled curse outside the tent had him instantly alert. It might have been the dream that unsettled him, or the fact that he was once again sleeping in a strange place, but he knew in his heart that there was evil within the camp. Slowly, Jonah rose so as not to disturb the intruders, guessing that they were armed and could injure one of his companions if they suddenly rushed from the tent.

Silently, Jonah made his way to the tent door. There he pulled the cloth that had slipped to his shoulders about his head. He bent his head, and in his mind said a prayer for courage and the safety of his mission. Then with one swift motion Jonah flung open the drape that covered the tent entrance and shouted, "Cease you, vipers of darkness!"

The early morning sun edged above the mountain to the east, and cast a sharp morning light directly into the small insignificant camp in the hills beyond Sidon. Its light filled the area and a beam seemed to shine directly on Jonah's face, creating a bright, white orb in the entrance of the tent. His sudden outburst caused all the bandits to freeze, and all the inhabitants of the camp to awake immediately. One of the bandits who had waited beside the tent saw Jonah's face in the bright light and recognized it as the face of the man who had lifted himself from the sand the day before when the bandit had stood on the bank and looked downward.

"It is the god from the sea!" he exclaimed in terror. He turned and began to race wildly back down the trail, repeatedly tripping and falling, then rising and running without regard to his injuries. The man beside him had sunk to his knees just as the men in the tent burst from it, pushing Jonah aside. Two other bandits fled, as much from being caught and outnumbered as from terror, and one more, the man who had never been a bandit before, but was a fisherman, tried unsuccessfully to hide in the bushes. After the turmoil that followed Jonah's stark appearance was sorted out, Darius found Jonah sitting peacefully on a rock.

"My father begins to appreciate that you have many abilities."

Jonah smiled. "Were any hurt?"

"No, but only two were polite enough to be captured. We will take them to Damascus, where my father will sell them as slaves."

"What if they have families?"

Darius shrugged. "One man pleads that his wife is about to deliver his fifth child."

"Darius, would you take me to your father?"

"My father would be pleased. He has hoped you would come to meet him, but has been afraid to ask since you showed your power this morning."

Jonah looked sideways at Darius with a scowl but said nothing more, just walked with him to where the second tent was being dismantled.

"Father," Darius spoke, approaching a tall man in a turban and long black robe who had his back to them. The man turned. He was a handsome man, browned by many years in the sun, with a short, brown beard that was streaked with gray. His dark eyes were sharp and his nose had a dominant ridge that seemed to reflect the straightness and firmness of the man's character.

Darius turned to Jonah but looked only at his father and said with pride, "This is my father, Kemuel, a master of trade and a descendant of the kings of Aram Damascus. Father, this is Jonah. He is the man that came from the belly of the great fish."

Kemuel stepped back and did not speak.

"Do not regard me as other than a man." Jonah stretched out his hand. "I travel to Nineveh because the God of heaven and earth has sent me, but I am only His servant."

Kemuel looked closely at Jonah, then stated flatly, "You will no longer be a bearer."

"I appreciate the reprieve." Jonah sighed with honest relief. "But I must earn my way because my purse was lost in the sea."

"You have averted a theft. That is enough until Damascus."

"Thank you, but who will replace me?" Jonah worried that the conversation would weary the busy man, but he felt obliged to continue on two accounts.

"One of the new slaves. They will travel with us to be sold in the market, or else I will take them as far as Harran." Kemuel turned as if the conversation was over.

"I would like to bargain for one of the men," Jonah said. He felt strongly that the man should return to his family.

Kemuel turned back, his face subtly different from before. Rather than a look of awe, there was cunning about the eyes of the merchant who had transacted many trades. "What do you offer?"

"I am not much of a porter, but I will continue until Damascus. From there, I can herd goats until Harran."

Darius had been watching curiously, but at this point he exclaimed, "Father, he is too weak to continue as a porter! Has he not served enough by preventing the robbery?"

Kemuel spun toward his son, obviously annoyed at the interruption. But his face softened for the briefest of moments before he turned again to Jonah.

"You may have one of the men for your service. You will not continue as a porter, but you will help with the goats beyond Damascus."

"Agreed," Jonah answered, but Kemuel was already walking away.

"Which man do you wish to serve you?" Darius asked.

"Bring me the one who spoke of his family," Jonah replied. "I will wait by that rock beneath the cedar grove. Be quick—the camp will be moving soon."

Darius ran off, only to return within minutes with a porter who led a man by a rope around his neck and whose hands were tied behind him. Jonah looked at the man's swollen face and knew there had been some brutality exerted. "You have a family," he stated.

The stooped man merely nodded.

"Yet you risked the welfare of your family by coming with this group of thieves to plunder that which you have not earned. There is no honor in such an act! A snake on his belly is the thief of the nest of the stork."

The defiant look in the eyes of the thief had faded and his head began to droop.

Jonah continued, "When you joined this band, you left your own family defenseless to be plundered by the darkness of a hard life where no father is there to provide for them. Your choices have led to the life you have. Because that life is no longer of joy to you, you think you can desert it and try another."

The man looked up sharply, clearly amazed that Jonah knew his heart. Jonah spoke with authority and sharpness.

"I tell you to go home, be a man, and make choices to improve your life, not abandon it." Then his voice softened, "Be kind to your wife, teach your sons, be gentle to your daughters, and give honor to the Lord God of heaven and earth that you are able to return to them."

The man began to sob and Darius gaped. "You do not wish

him to serve you? You are willing to continue to serve my father so that this man who tried to rob us in the night may return to his family?"

"The Spirit speaks to me that this man is not a thief," Jonah said. "Now cut him loose. I have found that a man who has made a mistake can change his life when given a second chance."

"Discredit not, O king, the tales of travelers," rejoined
the astrologer, gravely, "for they contain precious rarities
of knowledge brought from the ends of the earth."

Washington Irving, *Tales of the Alhambra*

Chapter Twelve

©©©©©©©©©©©©©

The climbs and descents of the journey were severe, and Jonah was thankful he no longer carried a burden, yet he still found it difficult to keep up with the younger men. The Abana River's source was a mountain lake to the north of where the guide led Kemuel and his small party through the steep-sided hills to Damascus. The party met the Abana River where it joined a spring in a more level valley. Here the party stopped for fresh water and a quick lunch. The sun neared its peak and the shadows of the canyons offered a welcome coolness that would be gone when they entered the desert plateau below, on which Damascus was built.

The mountain spring was icy cold, and each man drank from it as if he had thirsted a long time. Some doused their heads, but there was no time for baths. Kemuel was impatient, as there were still miles to travel before dusk. With the spring doubling the flow of the Abana, the river rushed quickly downward through a deep gorge its waters had carved out through the years. Here the party left the river because of the steepness and narrowness of the gorge, but even as they traveled a parallel canyon they could hear the roar of the river rushing downward until it escaped into the meadow lakes it fed. Through irrigation and the wise use of the Abana's water and its seven branches, a rich oasis on the edge of the Great Desert had been created. This oasis boasted great orchards of olive trees and well-tended gardens. Jonah followed the party through the orchards and fields, marveling at the wonderful network of canals and ditches that brought life and beauty to the area.

Darius rode near Jonah as he walked, and they talked of Damascus and the kingdom of Aram Damascus, of which the city was the capital. Jonah asked if Darius knew that Abraham had lived in Damascus for a time and perhaps even ruled there. Darius had heard this, as well as the claim that Abraham's chief servant, Elizer of Damascus, would have been Abraham's heir had Isaac and Ishmael not been born. Jonah wondered aloud if there were still remains of the garrison King David had built, but Darius suspected there were not. The desert winds and the constant rebuilding of a city that was strategically tempting to invading armies left little evidence of the past.

Finally, Jonah turned the conversation back to Darius. "You mentioned that your father was a descendant of the line of the kings of Aram Damascus."

"Yes, he is of the family of Hadadezer, King of Aram Damascus, who was leader of the twelve kings that fought against Shalmaneser III of Assyria. Seven times he fought against Assyria and triumphed."

Jonah suspected this was the version of history told in Damascus, and he had not seen Darius look so proud.

Then the boy sighed and continued, "My father's father had

an older brother, however, that was the oldest son and became king. Still, my father is of the royal family, and it is always good to return to Damascus."

The group had made camp one more night in the hills, but because of the descent and an early start the next day, they arrived at Damascus shortly before noon. The city was built on the south bank of the Abana River.

As the small party approached the western gate to the city, Darius moved his mule to the front and remained close to his father as they entered the walled fortress beneath the ancient arch. The excitement in Darius' face had increased the closer they had come to the city until Jonah was aware that he no longer followed the conversation; therefore, he had not been surprised when Darius had suddenly left him. This also left Jonah with more opportunity to observe the busy city, which was a major stop on the caravan routes from Egypt to Assyria. The streets of Damascus were narrow and twisted, but running from the west gate deep into the city, was a winding street lined on both sides with shops and bazaars crowded together and vying for prominence.

As they passed through the markets of the town, riding slowly over the dry streets, people stopped their chatter and bowed as Kemuel rode by. Occasionally, a richly dressed merchant would call out a greeting, and even more rarely, Kemuel would respond. But Jonah lost interest in his traveling companions as the smells of cooking food and the exotic items of hammered metal or the rich textures of woven rugs caught his attention. Momentarily, when he saw a piece of cloth that would be a good gift for his granddaughter, Adira, he wished he had his purse with him and was not dependent for everything on a youth and the grace of his father. But then Jonah reminded himself that in all things he was dependent on the Great Creator, who had given him life and the means to fulfill the work he was called to do. Furthermore, he had more than he needed by traveling with a wealthy, powerful man.

Kemuel had led the group since they left the mountain passes, no longer relying on the guide. He had paid the guide, and though the man still traveled with them, when they reached the city the guide went his own way.

Kemuel stopped now and turned to Darius. "Take the porters to the south gate where the caravan will be waiting, and have Lazar come to me after he has seen to the cloth. Warn him that the new slave needs to be shackled."

Darius readily agreed, obviously delighted with being entrusted with this errand. He led the porters away down a narrow street. No one had considered Jonah, but since his being there was due more to Darius than his father, he followed that way. Going southeast, they followed roads, though more correctly they were wide paths through the city. Some of the paths were wider than others, some led to more bazaars, and some narrowed into mere squeezes between houses and other buildings. When a path ended, sometimes the party headed left, sometimes right. Yet Darius clearly knew the way. There were obstacles: women with baskets or jars on their heads, men with bundles on their backs, and many dirty, barefooted children running about and laughing. Once they had to retreat in a narrow alley to allow a donkey with its burden to pass.

Near the south gate to the city was a large bazaar and beyond it the walled caravanserai, the inn for caravans. Darius passed through the arch into the area filled with tents, animals, sharp-tongued men, and worn, bent women stirring steaming pots. The walls of the caravanserai were lined by low-roofed stone buildings that served as sheds for the animals as well as rooms for the men who tended them. There was a strong smell of camel dung, rich spices, dirty robes, goat's milk, and dinners cooking. Jonah missed the coolness and fresh air of the mountains, forgetting the agony of the steep trails. He took a swallow from the skin Darius had given him for his water, but it was already warming in the desert sun. It would be a long time before he tasted fresh, cold water again.

Darius approached one of the dark, smelly buildings. "Lazar," he called, "Kemuel has arrived."

A very tall, black man emerged from the stone shed, ducking his head to clear the lintel of the doorway. "Darius!" he exclaimed.

Darius went forward and the two embraced.

"When did you arrive?" Darius asked.

"Two days ago. We traveled swiftly and all are enjoying the rest. Did your father obtain the cloth he sought in Sidon?"

Darius pointed toward the bundles. "When you have seen to this, my father wishes you to come to him. We were set upon by thieves the first night. This man" —Darius indicated a man who stood behind the other porters— "is a new slave. Keep him in shackles."

Lazar bowed deeply and moved over to the porters. When he saw Jonah standing among them, he called after the retreating Darius, "What of this one?" he asked, pointing at Jonah.

Darius turned back, a look of surprise on his face. "You did not go with my father?"

Jonah bowed his head.

"You better come with me now. I am sure they would enjoy meeting the 'god from the sea' at the palace." Darius grinned. "First, we both need to bathe and wash our clothing. Perhaps you can tell one of your stories tonight at dinner."

They worked their way back through the city, with Darius still riding the donkey. They arrived at the northern wall and passed through a narrow gate that led directly to the river. It had taken over two hours to deliver the porters and cloth to Lazar. Jonah looked toward the river and imagined the cool water on his sore feet. In an area where water had been diverted to create a large pool, women were beating laundry against stones. A herd of goats drank from the eastern bank of the pool, their hoofs sticking in the mud and grasses. Darius led the way to the western side where some stones created a smaller, cleaner area. He removed his clothes and plunged into the icy, clear waters. Jonah followed his example and jumped. The icy water sucked the air from his lungs, bringing a memory of his plunge into the dark sea from the ship of Tarshish. But this time his feet felt the sandy bottom and he pushed himself upward until his head was above the water. He gasped again and again until he could breathe normally. He glanced to where Darius was climbing from the pool to dry on a rock in the hot sun.

The lad grinned back at Jonah. "This is the River Abana that we followed in the mountains, and even with the heat of the sun, it never really warms up."

Jonah began awkwardly paddling his way to the side of the pool.

"I thought you came from the sea. How did you survive when you swim like that?"

Jonah pulled himself onto a rock. "I didn't swim. I told you, I was swallowed by a fish that later vomited me upon the shore. However, as a boy I used to swim in the sea. I spent several years in Zarephath, which is south of Sidon. But my mother took me to live with my grandfather when I was about your age. It was a farm, far from the Great Sea. Sometimes we went to the Sea of Gennesaret and I swam there. But that was many years ago. I am an old man now, so I swim like an old man."

"Is it harder to swim in a river or in the sea?"

"I have never swam in a river."

"Come on, let's get cleaned up. They'll have a great meal for us at the palace." Darius slid back into a shallow area and began to dip his clothes in the water, rub them together, beat them on a rock, and then repeat the process until the worst of the travel stains were dissolved.

The wall around the palace was as tall as the city wall. Though not as thick, the palace wall was much better built, with the stones set together tightly and no sharp edges protruding. The arch sat on two pillars, each of which featured an elaborately carved sphinx in bas-relief set into the front. Each sphinx had a man's head, a long beard, and a double crown on its head.

Darius noted Jonah's examination of the carvings and said, "My ancestor King Hazeal had the carvings done. He also built the Temple of Hadad. That is the first building over there." He pointed to the right of the road that led through the palace complex. It was a square, two-story building with two doors that stood open in the front. A slight glow as from small lamps came from within.

"Which god is Hadad?"

"He is the storm god—the god of Damascus and of the Aramaeans," Darius recited as if it was a lesson learned long ago, but he was distracted and he looked toward a group of buildings straight ahead. "Come, we will be late for dinner. The sun is setting quickly."

There was no challenge at the gate to the palace, for the guards recognized Darius as Kemuel's son, indicating the frequency with which Kemuel and his son came to Damascus. The various people within the complex all bowed shortly, but Darius appeared oblivious. He urged his donkey forward at a quicker pace, and Jonah found himself moving at a brisk trot to keep up.

The palace of Damascus, like many mideastern palaces, was composed of several buildings built around a central courtyard. The complex was large for such a small kingdom, due to the great wealth that passed through the city. The bazaars of Damascus were always busy, and even lazy or foolish businessmen could prosper. The king was wise enough not to tax too heavily the inhabitants of his kingdom, and to tax the caravans that passed through only slightly less than some cities on the route did, but more than most as it was still the quickest way to Harran and the Assyrian Empire.

The courtyard was sunken, with wide steps descending the four sides, and the corners and the central section were filled with gardens that produced a heavy scent of the flowers that drooped from bushes and trees, and spread along the ground. There was the sound of water from hidden fountains that were fed by water diverted from the river. Darius led Jonah along the left side of the courtyard to a building with many steps leading up to a pillared porch. He dismounted and ran up the steps to the doorway centered between two pillars. There he removed his sandals and a servant bathed his feet before providing him with clean sandals. Jonah was similarly cared for.

They passed inside to a room filled with the glow from hundreds of oil lamps. The lamps emitted light that was reflected by plaques of polished tin behind each, sending dancing rays throughout the room. The light glided over the pillars, the carvings, the golden vessels, and the rich fabrics that covered the floor, casting living shadows and creating dark corners. As his eyes better adjusted, Jonah saw that the room was filled with men who reclined on elaborately embroidered cushions around a large spread of roasted meats, fresh baked breads, dried fruits, cheeses, olives, and vessels filled with wine. Kemuel sat on a dais to the right of a man who was seated on higher cushions and wore silk robes. That man also wore several precious gems set in intricate gold bands and chains. Darius went forward slowly, then bowed at the base of the dais.

His father beckoned to him and offered his outstretched hand. Darius mounted two steps so he could take his father's hand, then he bent over it and murmured, "My apologies for being late."

"My son, Darius," he father said, introducing him to the man at his left, who Jonah had guessed must be the king, a cousin to Kemuel.

The man held out a hand that was dominated by a large ruby ring. "I beg your pardon, my king, for my delay," Darius repeated, going so low before the man that his forehead touched the floor. "But I have brought a man with me who came from the belly of a fish in Sidon. Some say he is a god of the Great Sea. I have brought him to entertain you because he is a gifted teller of stories."

The king looked to where Jonah knelt near the entrance of the room. "You may sit beside your father," was all he said, but he did not seem displeased. The men next to Kemuel nudged others down from the dais until a space was cleared. Two golden platters were brought, and Darius beckoned for Jonah to join him.

During the meal, Jonah told a story of life on the ark during the Great Flood. He amused the people with the antics of a thieving goat and a stubborn camel. But though he was preoccupied with the story and the task of entertaining his host, he noticed when a servant dropped a small piece of animal skin into Darius' lap.

When the story ended, more wine was brought and some

girls began dancing. Darius excused himself and Jonah made a similar plea to be allowed to retire early, then quickly followed behind his young master.

He entered the porch in time to see Darius pause to examine the piece of leather by the light of the moon. A puzzled look crossed his face and then he glanced around as if looking for someone. Then he cautiously began to move toward the sunken gardens toward the south.

"Darius," Jonah spoke softly.

Darius spun to see Jonah coming down the steps, but he did not speak.

"What has happened?" Jonah asked.

"It is a message from my sister." Darius held up the skin for Jonah to see. Burned into it with a stylus was the rough representation of a dove.

"What does it mean?"

"She would only send for me if there was danger. She lives in the women's quarters where she is preparing to marry the king's son. I must go to her." Again Darius began to walk rapidly across the courtyard, and this time Jonah followed.

On the south side of the courtyard, they turned east and passed several buildings that lined the gardens. Then, where there was a narrow alley between two buildings, they turned again to the south. The alley ended in a smaller courtyard surrounded by two-story buildings—the women's quarters.

A guard stopped them at the point of a spear.

"I am Darius, son of Kemuel. My sister is betrothed to the king's son. She has sent to see me," Darius said with feigned authority.

The guard called for another to come, then, while he held them in place, he sent the second guard for information. It was several minutes before the second guard returned. He delivered a message softly to the first, who turned to the two men and pronounced, "Your sister is very ill. She cannot be seen."

Jonah knew something was terribly wrong, and from the look on Darius' face, he could tell the boy felt the same. A strong prompting caused him to speak. "Darius," he whispered, "If I could see your sister, I might be able to save her."

Darius looked sharply at Jonah, but Jonah returned his look with a steady gaze and slowly nodded his head. Darius then spoke to the guard abruptly, "You will have my sister placed onto a bed and brought to me here, now!" The guard looked confused. "If I have to appeal to the king and interrupt his entertainment, he will not be pleased with your delay."

Finally, after more arguing and a large bribe that Darius had produced, his sister was brought out, lying on a bed carried by two old men.

An hour later, his sister was sitting up on the bed. Darius made his farewells with several cautions for her to follow regarding food and drink. She smiled and assured him that she knew the dangers of life in a palace.

"I was careless, brother, but I will be vigilant from now on. You must take care of yourself so that I will see you at the wedding feast next month."

Darius watched while she was carried away. Then he turned to Jonah as they walked back toward the main courtyard of the palace. "How is it you were able to heal my sister?"

"Many years ago, a great prophet named Elisha anointed me with the power of the Lord God. It is through that power that I can do all things, if it is his will."

Darius stopped. "If you have such power, why were you swallowed by a fish?"

Jonah halted, then laughed heartily. "Even a prophet can make mistakes. I made a very big mistake. I thought I could run away from the Lord God."

"So to punish you, your god sent a large fish to swallow you up?"

"No," Jonah said as he sat down on a low wall near a fountain. "The fish stopped me from doing the wrong thing. It gave me time to recognize that I had made the wrong choice. Then it set me back on the right course again. And, actually, the fish saved my life, for I would have drowned had it not come along."

"So your god is not vengeful?" Darius asked.

Jonah was not sure how to answer. He had always believed that the Lord met out justice to the children of men. Yet Jonah knew that he had not done anything to deserve a second chance. When Jonah had given the thief a second chance, he had not considered that he might be thwarting justice. It had just seemed the right thing to do. Did mercy rob justice? The thought was perplexing.

Darius now splashed at the fountain. "Come on," he called. "I'm tired. Let's go find where we are to sleep."

Dogs bark but the caravan moves on.

Arab Proverb

Chapter Thirteen

~~~~~~~~~~~~~~~~~~~~~~~~~~~~~~~~~~

*J*onah had seen few caravans, and none up close. The sheer size of it astounded him. Kemuel was majority owner of this caravan, with seven hundred camels. With one man in charge of eight to ten camels, all strung in a row, he hired over seventy men as camel masters. In addition, there were large herds of goats that provided milk, cheese, and occasionally meat for the men of the caravan. The goat herds traveled to the right or left of the main road where possible, but when they passed through areas where they had to join the main caravan, they fell in behind the camels. Last of all were the women, who tended to the milking, the preparation of meals, and the laundry, though most of the men just wore the same clothes until a special occasion called for a change; then they might send the travel-worn garment to be cleaned. The women also drove donkey-pulled carts filled with essential pots and supplies. At the back of the caravan, the women had the most unsavory road to travel, having to walk where animals had walked. Because of the number of camels, the road was covered with their droppings. Unable to avoid the smelly ground cover, the women just plodded through it.

It took all morning to depart from Damascus, and when the last of the women passed through the gate, Kemuel, on the lead camel, was a mile north into the desert. The shouting of men giving commands about loading goods onto camels, and at night directing the anchoring of ropes and the hoisting of tents; the gossip of women as they plodded along, or during stops, milked goats or prepared meals; the braying of camels; the bleating of goats; the harsh jangle of bells around the animals' necks; and various other sounds all combined to create a cacophony of noise that never ceased. The smells of the animals, of dirty, unwashed people, of dung heaps, and of moldy cheeses became familiar to Jonah. And though the smells were pungent and even foul, he reminded himself that they were not unbearable compared to the smells in the belly of the fish, because sometimes the cool spring breeze from the mountains would swirl around and carry the odors away. However, the dust and the flies were a new annoyance, the first getting into Jonah's clothes, ears, beard, and nostrils, and the second trying to.

He became intrigued with the ugly camels that were in the process of molting their winter coats. He would watch them with their patchwork fur and their awkward gate of both feet on one side moving in tandem: first one side, then the other, the loads swaying with the side-to-side motion. They were large animals with small, bony heads that always seemed to be tilted up proudly with their noses thrust into the air. Then Jonah noticed that it wasn't that the nose was high up, but that the eyes were set low in a direct line between the nostrils and the ears. Over the eyes was a ridge bone that helped shade the eyes from the bright desert sun. Then there was the double row of extra-long, thick lashes. One of the men who tended the camels explained that they had a third, clear eyelid that wiped across the eye, clearing away sand and dust, and that in a storm this eyelid could cover the eye completely, allowing the camel to continue to travel through blowing sand. The camels had wide, firm pads on their feet that spread out, allowing them to walk on the soft sand without sinking. They could travel days without food and on little water. They were much better suited to desert life than people, Jonah reflected wryly.

Jonah had to adjust to the vast emptiness of the desert that stretched cleanly in all directions, and to the ever-present glare of the sun bouncing off the sand, which seemed to pierce his soul. The intense light, the absolute heat, and the vast blue sky had a purifying effect. It stripped away concerns for the inconsequential and left him to ponder the lives stretching through the generations of men that had previously traveled through this desert. The scale of everything—the endless sand, the all-encompassing sky, and the encircling horizon—was massive, and even the large caravan seemed insignificant in comparison.

At night, when the heavens were filled with stars from horizon to horizon, Jonah pondered his own smallness in the vast universe. He could hardly believe he was traveling through this strange land to Nineveh to do as the Lord had called him to do.

Jonah adapted to life in a caravan, herding goats by day and sleeping on the hard ground at night. He was assigned to a herd of goats with two young lads. They mingled the does with the bucks because it was spring and the bucks were not troublesome. However, several does were ready to birth, and Jonah had to keep a constant watch in case one strayed away to deliver her kid.

The once-fresh clothes Darius had obtained for Jonah while in Damascus became smelly and caked with dust, and Jonah coughed constantly. By the second day, he had quit caring if the goatskin from which he and the two boys drank their water was clean or not. By the third day, Jonah was so exhausted that he fell asleep instantly at night or anytime the caravan stopped, yet woke suddenly if a goat bleated in agony during a difficult birth.

On the fourth night, when he had bedded down in the sheepskin Darius had given him, Jonah was about to close his eyes when a familiar voice beside him said, "Now would be a good time for you to tell me the story of the dividing of the Red Sea."

Jonah sat up to see Darius sitting back on his heels, an expectant expression on his face. Jonah ran his hand through his beard and sat up, looking briefly to where the goats slept like small stones upon the sand.

"Do you not sleep?" he asked wryly.

"You promised me a story."

With a smile, Jonah adjusted his back against a rock. Then he took a drink from the nearby goatskin and began. "Among all the many slaves of Pharaoh, none were as industrious as the Hebrews. But none troubled him as much, either. The Hebrews worked hard because they believed it was right for a man to always do his best, but they also believed that one day God would send them a deliverer and they would be free from Pharaoh's decrees and abuses."

So Jonah sat in the midst of a caravan about to travel into the territory of the wicked Assyrians and told the story of how God miraculously spared His people from the wicked Egyptians. Darius asked many questions, forcing Jonah to search his memory to fill in the details he had forgotten. Which plague came first? What were the names of the tribes? The boy's questions were endless. The camp was quiet when Jonah at last lay down and fell quickly to sleep.

Three days later, the caravan arrived within sight of Tadmor, known as the city of dates. It was a vital stop for travelers crossing the Syrian desert, and in Aramaic its name meant "the indomitable city."

Clearly anticipating the rest and fresh water of the city, the members of the caravan began to pick up their weary pace. It was just past midday and they would be there within the hour, well before the time when the women would prepare dinner. Jonah thought of how it would feel to sleep the extra hour or two the early stop would offer.

Suddenly, Jonah noticed that the camels in the train to his right were becoming restless. Several men near the animals looked around with obvious concern.

Then there was the call that sent a chill down Jonah's spine and sent the caravan into a state of panic. "Storm!" a lone voice rang out.

Every head turned toward the sky, and Jonah saw a growing darkness on the eastern horizon. A massive storm of sand billowed toward them, and though it was still several miles off, it would be upon them in minutes. Each man in charge of a train of camels immediately leaped onto the lead camel and kicked the animal into a run toward the city.

Jonah called to the boys who helped him, and they ran to the rear of the goats and began to drive them toward the city in a frenzy of shouts and of lashes with long sticks. With no time to chase every stray goat, they concentrated on the main herd while the razor-sharp sand began to pelt their hands. The women, who usually walked behind the caravan to manage carts pulled by donkeys, began to run past, screaming in terror. Some stayed with the carts and, by climbing on the carts or mounting the donkeys, soon had the beasts so overburdened that the donkeys refused to move despite repeated beatings.

Ahead, men of the city of Tadmor had opened the great Bashan wood gates and were issuing forth to help the caravan before it became engulfed in the quickly closing storm.

Even as he ran for the goats, Jonah had wrapped his face with the cloth that hung from his head, but the air continued to thicken with sand swirled up by the wind. He peered through the thinnest slits possible, yet sand began to sting at his eyes. The poor, dumb beasts in his charge bleated in fright, but they continued to move to avoid the lash of the sticks.

As the edge of the main storm hit, Jonah and his herd passed through the city gates. He was directed toward a low building and it wasn't until the door was shut that he realized how loud the wind had been. Standing in the relative silence of bleating goats, he removed the cloth from his face. When his eyes adjusted to the gloom, he looked around to see his two helpers, plus several other boys that herded goats in the caravan. Each stood like an island in a sea of angry goats. It would take hours to sort out the herds again.

Relieved that they had made it to shelter, Jonah began to laugh. One by one the lads joined him, while tears washed the grit from their stinging eyes. Then they all gratefully shared the water skins.

The storm passed and sunlight streamed in the door. Though the storm had brought the darkness of a moonless night, it was a bright day again. After he tended to the goats, Jonah left the low shed to see how the rest of the caravan had fared.

Entering the main court of the caravanserai, Jonah looked around. Tadmor had been built by King Solomon. Jonah hoped he'd have time to explore the city and to speak to the old men who remembered best the ancient tales. The thick walls of the city were made of brick, as were most of the buildings. There were wooden lintels and doors, but few windows because sand would blow right through the latticework.

People and animals from the caravan had crowded into stables and sheds when they rushed into the city, seeking refuge from the storm. But now that the storm was past, many people had emerged and were picking up debris and organizing the upset supply carts. Women were already building fires, shaping flat bread, and preparing stew. Several goats had died in the storm, and their bodies were being recovered. There would be fresh meat tonight.

As Jonah drank from the cool water of the well, a man rushed up to him. "Is Darius not with you?" he asked with desperation on his face.

Jonah spun around to see Darius' main servant. "No, isn't he with his father?" Jonah knew the answer before he asked.

"He has not been seen since before the storm."

Jonah rushed toward the gates that had been opened as soon as the storm moved past. Just inside the gates, Kemuel sat on a horse, surrounded by six other men on horseback. He was giving orders, and they rode out before Jonah could reach them.

Standing in the opening, Jonah gazed at the barren landscape. All traces of the caravan's passing had been obliterated, except for a couple of mounds that men were rushing to investigate. In such a storm, Jonas knew that Darius could be anywhere, buried until another ferocious wind blew the sand away and uncovered his dry bones.

Jonah looked toward the blue sky, with the late afternoon sun beginning to set behind the city. "O Lord, Jehovah, maker of seas and sand, ruler of the stars, the mountains and the desert, hear my prayer. A young lad has been lost in the turmoil of the storm. Darius has been my friend and my protector, and through him I have been able to do thy will in traveling toward Nineveh. Help me, I pray to find him!"

After his prayer, Jonah stood with his head bowed and became very still. He cleared his mind, slowed his breath, and waited. Finally, he lifted his head and called to a servant who stood nearby, watching him.

"Bring water quickly," was all he said.

The servant ran to the well and returned shortly with a goatskin still wet from the filling. Jonah and the servant passed through the gates and walked along the western city wall, not pausing to inspect the many mounds and drifts. They plodded through the deep, fresh sand that had blown up against the wall, sometimes sinking to their knees, sometimes reduced to crawling. At the end of the wall a large tower protruded, its straight sides causing Jonah to adjust his course, but he continued to circumvent the city, the servant following him. After turning north along the western wall, Jonah began to run because the sand drifted away from the wall here and the ground was firm. Then, at a misshaped mound in the smooth wave of sand that arched away from the wall, Jonah fell to his knees and began to dig.

A large cloth made from camel hide covered a still figure. Jonah pulled back the hide and there lay Darius, curled up tight and sound asleep.

Later, Darius told how he had dismounted and then become disoriented in the storm, and unable to find either his camel or the gate, had headed for the shelter of the western wall. There he had done as he had been taught to do in such a situation. And, once out of the fury of the storm, he had done what young boys do who must lay still for a period of time. He napped. He had not considered that he might run out of air, or that he might not have been found. His biggest worry was that his father would be angry that he had gotten off his camel.

"I dropped a knife my father gave me. I knew I would not find it when the storm passed," he explained as they walked slowly back toward the city gate.

That night, the entire camp rejoiced at the miraculous recovery of the master's son. No human lives had been lost, and the loss of animals had been minimal—only a half dozen goats. Two camels had become so entangled that when they could not be quickly cut free, they had been abandoned. When the storm passed, they were found outside the city, where they were cut free, taken within, and rewarded for their foolishness with copious amounts of water.

After a delicious meal, Kemuel sent for Jonah to thank him for finding and saving his son, but he learned that Jonah had retired to his bed and was sound asleep.

The next day, carts and equipment were repaired. Goats roamed in the grasses of the oasis, and Darius ran about the bazaars of the city with the recklessness of a youth who has narrowly escaped a fatal accident. He came upon Jonah, who was sitting beneath a tree near a fountain.

Darius ran and sat down on the fountain wall beside his older friend. "How did you know where to find me after the storm?"

"I prayed, and the Lord God told me in my mind."

The boy paused and then asked, "Does your god speak to everyone?"

"To everyone who asks and will listen."

"Is that why you are going to Nineveh? Did you ask your god what you should say to them?"

"Well, not exactly. The Lord God will give answers to all who ask as it concerns their lives. But to a few he gives answers concerning many. These are called prophets, and to them he gives commandments for his prophet to speak to all."

Darius was quiet for a while, stirring the water of the fountain with his finger. Then he looked up into Jonah's eyes. "So you are a prophet?"

"Yes."

"And you have been told to go to Nineveh?"

"Yes, to tell the people there that they need to repent." Jonah's voice was soft.

"But you have not been told to tell my people to repent?"

The lad's question was unexpected. "No, but do not be discouraged. A prophet may come yet."

Darius looked at him sharply, but Jonah's eyes twinkled. With a burst of laughter, Darius rose and ran off into the busy bazaars.

Later that evening, Darius made another appearance, this time handing Jonah a cake of freshly baked bread and a chunk of cheese before demanding the story of Abraham. And so, between bites, Jonah told him how God commanded Abraham to sacrifice Isaac. Darius was disturbed by the story, even though Jonah tried to explain that it was about obedience. But how was he to properly explain obedience when he had run from God?

"Where is your father?" Jonah asked, changing the subject.

"He sits with his advisers and scouts." Darius shrugged.

"The boys who herd goats with me say your father is very wealthy. How many of the goats and camels of this caravan are his?"

"Seven hundred camels. His animals carry Phoenician

glass and ornaments of silver, gold, and copper. They carry the purple cloth of the Phoenicians you carried from Sidon and fabric from Lebanon with its beautiful embroidery, which is so precious it is packed in chests of cedar wood. On the way home after trading, the camels will carry spices and rugs and other items we obtain. It has taken years, but this year he is wealthy."

Astonished, Jonah asked the question that had bothered him since he had learned that Darius' father owned his own caravan. "Why did you hire me? Certainly he had enough boys already."

"Of course. But I am old enough to begin my own business," Darius replied. "This trip you trade your stories to travel in the safety of our caravan. When you tend goats, I make a double profit because you replaced a boy who became ill at Dor. My father gives me the items of trade to pay the boys after my share. I keep your portion."

"What do I get for tending goats?" Jonah asked.

"My company and protection within the caravan. No one will bother you because I am the son of the master."

Again Jonah was astonished. He had not considered his own safety, but he now realized it was a good trade. He was traveling into the Assyrian Empire, and the Assyrians had long been the enemy of his people. Without protection, he could have been in great danger.

Darius kicked at the sand. "The people also fear you because they have heard that you were spit up on the beach by a large fish. Some believe you are a god from the sea."

Jonah looked sideways at him. "Where have they learned of this?"

Darius shrugged as he walked away. "People talk." He glanced back at Jonah.

Jonah just shook his head as he rose to quiet some restless goats. It was late when he retired to his bed.

Two days later they arrived at Resafa, more of a military fort than a city. The Assyrians had built it and maintained an army there. On the edge of the desert, Resafa was too far from the Euphrates to have a spring or natural running water. Large cisterns were sufficiently filled during the rainy seasons to supply the outpost with water throughout the year. Caravans stopped at the city to purchase water. The main body of soldiers was not currently in Resafa, so the day the caravan spent there was peaceful, used mostly to refill water containers.

Upon leaving Resafa, the caravan entered the great plain of the Kharbur-Euphrates watershed. They began to see exotic game—deer, partridge, and quail—which occasionally found its way into their evening meals. Nomads with great flocks of sheep maintained a discreet distance from the caravan, often appearing as nothing more than dots on the landscape.

After they carefully crossed the Euphrates River at Circesium, the caravan's pace slowed. Here the route divided, passing southeastward along the course of the great river down toward the far-distant Babylon, or north to Harran. Some caravans would bypass Harran on the way to Nineveh by choosing a route north to Gozan instead, but Harran was such a major trade city that most caravans followed the road northwest along the Khabour River. From Harran, the road went east to Gozan and beyond along the Sinjar mountain range toward Nineveh.

They camped at the crossing, and the next day they followed the Euphrates for a time before leaving it for the Khabour River, the last major tributary to join the Euphrates. The next day, they camped a day's journey from Harran. The caravan had been on the road for weeks now; summer was coming upon them and Kemuel was driving them as quickly as he could. The plan was to get back to Damascus before the dry season intensified.

Ever dusty and thirsty, Jonah rose from his bed stiff and bruised. He kicked the rock that had stuck in his back during his sleep and then rolled up his sheepskin. The closer they came to Harran, the more he had pondered the story of Abraham, whose father, Terah, had taken his family there after leaving Ur. Until this trip, Jonah had not fully appreciated the great distance that journey had entailed.

It was shortly after the noon stop when Darius found Jonah and walked beside him near the goats.

"We will arrive in Harran before the sun sets," Darius said. "Is this not where Abraham came for a while?"

Jonah looked at him. "You seem to know more about Abraham than I have told you."

"Yes." Darius nodded. "He lived in this land."

"But you asked for stories as if you had never heard them."

"You tell the stories very well. You know them better than others," Darius said with a wave of his hand.

Jonah began to wonder if Darius was older than he had assumed.

"Now tell me about when Abraham traveled to Egypt because of the famine."

Jonah sighed and told the story as it had been recorded in the ancient record.

The last hour of the journey took them through a flat, dry plain with no trees. In the middle of this wasteland, the caravan city of Harran rose. From Harran, the trade route stretched to another ford on the Euphrates River at Carchemish, fifty-five miles to the west. From there it continued to ports on the Great

Sea. To the east, the route stretched along the foothills of the Sinjar Mountains to Nineveh and the Orient. The Khabour River route they had followed came from the south, bringing traffic from as far away as Ur. Each route was regularly filled with caravans, and all roads paused in the wilderness at Harran, the great crossroads, which was nourished by many wells.

Jonah and those he traveled with were still three miles from the city when a great stir passed through the caravan. Jonah saw Darius hurrying toward him, looking worried.

"What has happened?"

"A rider has just arrived," the lad said as he approached, nearly out of breath. "Soldiers of Nineveh are approaching Harran from the west. It is the army from Resafa returning to their fort. We will stop here in this gully along the river and be still."

"Why does a whole caravan stop because of a few soldiers?"

Darius looked aghast at the question, then said simply, "Come, I will show you."

He led the way up a hill that had hidden the view to the northwest. He lay flat on the top, and Jonah lay down also. Harran was a great, circular city built around a hill. On the top of the hill was a great temple that could be seen from without the city walls. Next to the nearest gate was a large palace. The city was even more impressive than Damascus. Then Jonah saw a large cloud of dust like a massive storm approaching from the route to Carchemish. The cloud seemed to rush toward the city like a disembodied monster.

"There are about two thousand men on horses," Darius exclaimed. "The rest of the army follows on foot a few miles behind."

He and Jonah watched as the horsemen rushed toward the

gates of Harran. Then they went back down the slope to where the caravan waited undetected.

"I have only seen such a group once before." Darius was visibly shaken. "It is not a good night to be in Harran. The soldiers do not like to be denied anything. We will wait until dark, when they are drunk, and then we will enter."

"Why do you not wait here?"

"It is dusk and the sun is setting, but in the light of morning when they travel back to Resafa, our camp would be directly in their path. It will be better to blend in with the city of Harran tonight after they have pillaged it and begun to sleep off their drunkenness. Still, much of our goods will be theirs."

"You will let them have your goods?" Jonah asked.

"They will not take everything. What else can we do? We have traveled far to trade at Harran."

"Why do you come here if such a thing is possible?" Jonah asked.

"Harran receives goods that are valuable in the south. It is a good place to trade." Darius did not look happy. "The soldiers are not here often. After they leave tomorrow, we will still trade before we turn toward the road south."

"You are not going all the way to Nineveh?" Jonah had not realized that soon he would be on his own in the middle of Assyrian territory. But Darius had not heard him.

"Excuse me," the boy said. "I would like to go be with my father now." With that, Jonah's small protector left.

Much later that night, the caravan began the three-mile journey to Harran. Every bell and every animal were muzzled. Stretched out single file, the caravan was more than a mile long. At the gate, the guard, who had been bribed earlier to expedite their entrance, slowly opened only one of the great doors. He silently directed them to where the caravansari was located to their right.

Despite the precautions, the caravan could not help but make some noise. The plodding of nearly a thousand camels and thousands of goats, plus the men, the creaky carts, the jangle of an unsecured iron pan, the moment when a chest fell and shattered on the cobbles, and the unstopped curse when a man's hand was smashed in trying to stop it, were sounds that could almost stop one's heart. Finally, they were all within the city walls, and only one drunken soldier had to be knocked on the head to silence him.

An hour later, Jonah cowered in the darkness of an open shed behind the goats in the relative safety of the caravansari as Assyrian soldiers from Resafa ranged through Harran, plundering and destroying at their pleasure. Most were drunk, filthy, and mean. They were men of war and had little regard for life. They spoke with loud voices, sang at the top of their lungs, laughed loudly at crude jokes, and shouted at everything. They carried long swords and wore thick boots. Though the caravan had waited to enter, the soldiers did not cease their temporary employment until the early hours before dawn. But none came to the caravansari because they clearly still thought it was empty.

The members of the caravan escaped the cruelty endured by those who had received the first assault from the soldiers. Still, Jonah and the others were chilled by the reports Lazar had brought after going ahead to pay the bribe for their entrance and the fees for their accommodations. In addition to the distant screams from women that the people of the caravan could hear, Lazar told of the brutality of the soldiers, the whimpering of children in hiding, and the near-silent acquiescence of men who meekly bowed and backed away. Horror and fear kept Jonah and his friends in a wakeful silence through the night. As the hours passed, the animals of the caravan became restless, straining at their muzzles and the ropes that kept them closely tied.

It was deep into the dark hours of a long night before exhausted sleep overtook the soldiers. Every building in Harran had been filled with soldiers except the temple—Ehulhul, temple of the pagan god Nannar, the moon god. Harran was the center of the cult, and the temple, prominent on the hill, was adorned by Assyrian governors and kings. The city was built to represent the shape of the moon, and all the roads, temples, and buildings were built to resemble the city of Ur, the other residence of Nannar.

Jonah had been unable to sleep, and when the sky finally became a pale grey just before dawn, he rose from his cramped position. He found himself walking through the mangled city, maneuvering around sleeping bodies and debris. He walked down narrow streets and passed by pools, some of which had stone altars rising up from them. Unknown to Jonah, in these pools the priests would swim as part of their daily devotions, surrounded by leaping, sacred fish. It was believed that some of the fish were so tame they would come to the priests if they called their names. Some in the city even believed the fish spoke to the priests, delivering messages from Nannar.

Curiosity caused Jonah to climb one of the roads leading to the temple at the top of the central hill. Though the sky was becoming a pale blue with the emerging sunlight, a great darkness seemed to engulf the pagan temple. Jonah backed away to where the shadows were less thick. In despair, he leaned against a tree and looked toward the pale sky in the east, just as the sun pierced the horizon. He found himself voicing a prayer.

"O God, the great Jehovah, I am alone in this land of

wickedness. There are unbelievers and false gods everywhere. There are bloodthirsty men and thieves. How am I to continue into the depth of this land? I have no purse. I have no companion beyond this city. I am not trained in defense, and my skills within a caravan are limited to the work of a boy. What have you asked of me?"

He stood in the failing darkness, feeling alone and forgotten, with the dark temple behind him and the empire of Assyria stretching into his future. Then, as the sun sent its first rays over the plain and over the city wall, Jonah felt peace. A warmth radiated through him, beyond the warmth of the sun, and he felt a voice speak to his heart: "I am the Lord thy God. With me all things are possible. Trust in me."

The caravan spent the next morning gathering men and animals, making contact with merchants, and conducting business very quietly in the dangerous calm while the soldiers slept. Jonah went to fill large jars at a well. He had just lifted one to his shoulder when he heard the approach of a familiar voice.

"Good morning to you, Jonah," Darius said casually.

Jonah looked at him and then began to walk toward the trough where he would pour the water for the goats. "I did not think I would see you again. I am glad you have come."

"I have been worried about you. You are not an Assyrian. You will be traveling a long way into a dangerous land."

"Yes, I will."

"They say in Nineveh the people sell their babies to the priests, who sacrifice them to their gods."

Jonah thought again of his granddaughter, Adira. "Yes, I have heard such tales before." A grimace crossed his face.

"I talked to my father. He is grateful to you. You have kept me company. He will talk to the merchant that travels with a caravan that is at Gozan. The man knew we were coming, and he came here to buy cloth from my father. He leaves tomorrow. Perhaps you will be able to tend goats for them." Darius had a grin on his face.

Jonah looked at him and saw that the boy was sincere. Then he looked to heaven and said aloud, "Forgive me, Jehovah. I should not have doubted."

Now Nineveh was an exceeding great city of three days' journey, and Jonah began to enter into the city a day's journey, and he cried and said, Yet forty days, and Nineveh shall be overthrown.

Jonah 3:3–4

Chapter Fourteen

❧❧❧❧❧❧❧❧❧❧❧❧❧❧

The new caravan Jonah had joined left Gozan within a week. Located on the Kharbur River, Gozan was a province of the Assyrian Empire and contained a small palace for the local governor. Jonah settled in with the goat herders as he had before, but he missed his small companion who would suddenly appear and demand a story. Sometimes he imagined what story he would have told the lad. He prayed for Darius, realizing he would probably never see the young man again.

A few days after leaving Gozan, the caravan arrived at Nisibis. Here Jonah learned that trade was conducted with much shouting, deception, and false promises. He had left Harran before the main trading had begun, but the sporadic trading along the way, conducted by Kemuel, had been done with few words and a great deal of presence by the master of the caravan, descendant of kings. However, Nisibis would not be the final destination, and most of the trading would occur in Nineveh. The city was surrounded by gardens and wooded with olive, fig, and other trees. Beyond this cultivated plot spread the broad expanse of the desert. A spring gushed out of a rock and supplied the inhabitants with water and irrigated their gardens, then flowed away to feed into the Kharbur. Despite the mayhem and posturing in the marketplace, it was a peaceful city.

The masters of the caravan took an extra day in Nisibis, and Jonah spent it in the hills north of the city in fasting and prayer, hoping to better prepare for his arrival at Nineveh.

The closer the caravan came toward Nineveh, the larger on the horizon the image of a large, flat-topped structure grew. It stretched south as far as Jonah could see, and as they neared it, he could finally discern that it was an enormous wall. The road led the caravan to a gate near the northern reach of the wall, and as they came even closer Jonah saw the Tigris River flowing between them and the great wall surrounding Nineveh.

A large caravansari had been built on this side of the river so that caravans from the west could conduct business without having to transport their goods across the Tigris. Here the caravan did its final trading before beginning its return journey to Harran, Carchemish beyond that, and perhaps as far as Alalakh, a port city on the Great Sea. Nineveh was a major city connecting the north-south trade with the east-west trade.

They spent the night in the caravansari, and when the master was no longer occupied with the many tasks involved in getting a caravan settled, Jonah approached him. He thanked the man for employing him as a goat herder, explaining that at first light he would cross the Tigris into Nineveh. The man directed one of his captains to pay Jonah for his time, and then Jonah found a place to sleep in one of the crowded, smelly sheds.

Early the next morning, Jonah went down to the river dock, where the loading of goods from the caravan had already begun. The spring flooding was past, and the Tigris had subsided closer to its low flow; it was now less than ten feet deep. From the south, smaller vessels and barges arrived at the dock, though traffic was sparse in the early morning light.

Tired of the chaos of caravans and trade negotiations, Jonah eagerly paid his passage on a barge. In addition to the coins he had received the night before, Jonah also had a small purse Darius had given him, safely tucked in his robes. The barge was full of bundles, jars, and other containers of precious goods, but the crossing went quickly, and Jonah soon clambered up the bank on the other side of the river.

Coming down to the river dock was a road that led directly to the gate that pierced the wall of Nineveh, and Jonah began following this road. Intersecting it was another stretching from the distant south to the far northern gate to his left, where it diminished to a path leading into the hills.

The road from the dock to the gate sloped upward, more like a long, wide ramp, and on it a continual flow of traffic moved smoothly, mostly made up of carts bringing goods from the dock into the city. Jonah followed behind a two-wheeled cart pulled by a mountain mule. He recognized some of the bundles of purple cloth he had escorted across the pass from Sidon to Damascus. That seemed so far away now. He was tired from the long journey from Sidon and walked with his head down, watching the road's pattern of stones beneath his feet twist and weave. He had arrived at his destination, but he was filled with an anticlimactic weariness that enveloped him. Then he looked up at the gate. The sun was still low in the eastern sky behind the city, and the shadow of the massive gate reached to darken much of the ramp leading up to it.

Jonah strained his neck to see the top of the gate as he climbed further toward it. The structure was made of bricks, and the underside rose up in a perfect arch so high that ten men could have stood on each other's shoulders beneath it. The painted designs covering the surface featured bright colors that seemed to glare at Jonah even in the shade. It was in that moment that Jonah realized the full scale of what he had to do. Just as the gate dominated everything beneath it, so the city of Nineveh was larger by far than any city Jonah had ever seen. And so was the Assyrian Empire, of which Nineveh was a major city, far larger than Israel, Judah, Syria, or any of the other kingdoms Jonah knew.

"Lord, give me strength," he prayed.

No greedy guards were collecting bribes from people before they could enter the city, but several soldiers, evenly spaced on either side of the road, stood silent and stern. Jonah wondered if he would ever be allowed to leave. All the traffic seemed to be entering the city. Jonah had not seen a sign of anything going down to the dock or the road to the south. Perhaps it was the caravan's arrival that dictated the direction of the flow. Then he entered the tunnel of the arch and felt a chill run down his arms. It was not the cool of the deeper shade he felt but the evil from the city within.

The road into the city stretched before him, wide and nearly straight. Clustered at the gate were girls in bright fabrics and sheer veils, leaning against the walls, trying to entice merchants and barge workers from the river to spend money on them. They had tattoos on their arms and rings in their noses. Tiny bells tinkled from their foreheads and arms. Hurrying by them and the men who stopped to talk to them, Jonah entered the city.

Inside the gate was a large bazaar filled with the usual vendors and crowds. But Jonah decided it would be more productive to get further into the city, and perhaps further south. He chose a large road leading east.

As he walked, he noticed various roads branching off, winding away to the left or the right. The road he was on became increasingly narrow and began to twist and branch until he realized he needed to abandon it and head south. The homes that were thick around the bazaar he had first passed through began to thin. He passed by a well-guarded grove of fruit trees and several homes sitting back from the road that were surrounded by gardens, pools, and fields of animals. The road he had chosen was wider than the one he had left, cobbled like the ramp leading into the city and edged by low walls, with few twists and no dramatic corners like the streets of Damascus and other smaller cities.

The people on this road traveled by foot, in carts, or on mule or horse. Many wore simple clothing made of wool, but others wore elaborate clothing with fringed hems made of embroidered fabrics from Lebanon or brightly colored silks—the fabric and dyes from India. Jonah even saw two people who wore the purple cloth from Sidon and who were adorned with bracelets, beads of glass, and earrings of silver and gold. Wealthy people traveled in covered chairs carried by bearers. They rode behind silk coverings, their chins up and their eyes forward, looking neither to the right nor to the left. A man going before one of these conveyances shouted when Jonah didn't move aside quickly enough, and the man fired a kick that fortunately missed Jonah's shin.

Jonah drank the rest of the water he carried in a goatskin and began to watch for a well. He ate the last of the dates and dried meat he carried. For hours he walked past vast estates, proud people, small markets, and busy servants rushing around on errands and to temples built to false gods. Jonah refilled his water skin at a central well in one of the markets, where he also sat for a rest. Then, feeling the need to continue, he began to walk again. As he approached one temple with large, carved beasts guarding its entry, he saw people lined up, swaying and chanting. They all wore the finest clothing, and some carried incense sticks that smoked in the breeze. They swayed before the temple Emashmash—the temple of Ishtar—as men from a nearby building approached. They wore dark robes, and some wore masks of animals such as a bull or lion. They represented the male divine who would worship and be worshipped by the woman who served as the goddess within. The people parted to let the men enter the temple before them, their chanting becoming louder and fiercer. Jonah sensed a feeling of intense evil, and he quickly passed on.

This was the great evil that Jezebel had brought to Israel. It permeated and corrupted the world, but the destruction of the faith of Jonah's own people was especially painful. They had had the truth, they had seen the power of God countless times, yet their passivity, vanity, and greed led them to reject the Lord and choose instead the sexual sins and human sacrifices the pagan gods required.

After walking for about an hour, Jonah saw another large market in the distance. The sun was lowering in the west, and soon the light would be blocked by the city wall. It was nearing the time for market stalls to close, and many people were out making purchases needed for the evening meal. The closer Jonah got to the market, the thicker the crowd became. People also streamed into the square from the west, where another large gate opened to the city. The docks emptied as men entered Nineveh for the night.

Many people had the look of faraway places. Some were dressed in tatters or rough robes; others bore the weight of chains, led like animals toward the market, to be sold as slaves. A boy with a twisted foot stood on a stone near the edge of the crowd, balancing himself with a crutch and crying in a hoarse voice to the crowd, "Carvings for sale. Beautiful animals carved in cedar." But no one seemed to even glance his way. He looked tired, as if he had stood there since dawn. A woman on a beautiful horse rode close by and knocked the boy backward from his perch, sending some of his carvings scattering beneath the feet of the crowd.

"Watch yourself, little beggar!" the woman snapped. "I won't have my horse smeared by your grimy hands."

Jonah tried to reach the boy, but by the time he arrived the lad had retrieved what he could and was gone.

Jonah looked westward at the orange sky created by the setting sun. He had traveled a day's journey into Nineveh, and still the city stretched beyond his sight. He felt weak, having fasted since he had finished his dates and dried meat that morning. His muscles were sore, though by now he was used to walking a full day, and his feet were hot. Suddenly, a far-off memory came to him. He lay on the beach of Sidon, still stinking from the great fish, and the Lord spoke to him again, "Arise, go unto Nineveh, that great city, and preach unto it the preaching that I bid thee." He knew the moment had arrived for him to do as he had been commanded.

Jonah proceeded to the center of the market. He could see booths similar to the one that Danawi, the merchant of Joppa, had used to sell his wares. He also saw stalls with produce that was brought in for the day; these stalls were smaller and nearly empty. The owners were already packing up to return to their farms to prepare for the next day.

There were stalls where the elaborate cloths and rugs of the world were sold. There were small alabaster plaques and carvings in wood and ivory. There were jewelry and scarves, veils and ornate sandals, ornaments for the hair, and rings for the fingers and toes. Jonah wandered through the alleys of the bazaar until he came to an area that opened in a large courtyard.

At one end of the courtyard was a stone-walled canal from which women were drawing water. At the opposite end of the courtyard was a stage, also of stone. Across the front stood large, upright beams with iron rings bolted to them. Attached to each ring were three or four thick, black chains. At the end of each chain was a man, bruised and nearly naked. This was a slave market. The crowd was thinning, and the man who sold the slaves was retiring for the day. He motioned to a large man who stood at the back of the stone platform, and they began to remove the chains from the rings and lead the remaining men away.

Jonah stood across the courtyard, heartsick at the wickedness of the people. The platform loomed above him, and as the last of the slaves and the slave trader exited, Jonah took a deep breath then mounted the stone steps at the side. He gazed out at the hurrying, passing people, cleared his throat, and began with a small, almost squeaky voice.

"People of Nineveh, the Lord God has commanded me to call you to repentance."

When no one even looked at Jonah, many thoughts went through his head. There was a faint hope that perhaps he had done enough and could now leave. Then, as he stood there in the dimming light of Nineveh, he remembered his time in the belly of the great fish. Vividly, he recalled the darkness, the foul smell, the slime, and the seaweed wrapped around his head. He remembered the long days of prayer and how he had offered his voice in giving thanks—the only sacrifice he had to offer. He recalled the moment when the fish had swept upward through the depths of the sea and had vomited him alive onto the sand at Sidon.

Jonah knew that it was only through the mercy of God that he now stood in Nineveh. This was his mission. There was no doubt about what he was to do. He had made his choice when the Lord gave him a second chance. Now he would fulfill his call as a prophet.

Jonah took a deep breath, stepped forward, and with a clear, strong voice began again. "People of Nineveh, listen to me. I have come a great distance to warn you. I have traveled through the sea in the belly of a great fish. I have crossed the hills, plains, and deserts undetected by my enemies. I have been delivered to bring you a message from the God who created heaven and earth. The Lord God has seen your wickedness and abominations. He has seen your pride and your vanities. He has sent me to cry unto you that in forty days the great city of Nineveh will be destroyed, except you repent!"

This time he gathered some attention. People began to stop and look at him. He mustered his courage and began again, even stronger, focusing on the fact that he had been saved from the belly of a great fish to preach to their city. More people gathered, but they clearly did not like the message of this strange man who spoke their tongue with a foreign-sounding voice.

"Go home, old man!" someone shouted.

"If you do not repent of your wickedness, this great city will be destroyed!" Jonah persisted.

"Who will destroy Nineveh? You and your army, old man?" another passerby asked in derision. "When will they arrive? Did you say forty days? Is it because they are older than you and don't travel as fast?"

The people laughed at him, but still he cried unto them. Unnoticed at the back of the crowd, a man in a richly embroidered yellow robe over a pale purple tunic listened intently. The man's hand rose to his white beard, and then he turned and climbed into a chariot. His aged hands lifted the reins with confidence, and the horses responded to the light whistle of their master. They trotted away into the deepening twilight. The flash of yellow at the back of the crowd briefly caught Jonah's attention as the man drove away.

Suddenly, Jonah was hit by a piece of stale bread and was momentarily stunned. But his call was greater than the ridicule of the people. As he began again, the people became a mob. Many hurried to nearby food stands, and soon Jonah was being pelted with overripe dates, hard animal dung, and cheese that had gone bad in the hot day's sun. Then, a hush spread over the crowd, and in the stillness Jonah heard the steady rhythm of marching feet. The crowd parted and ten soldiers approached the stand. One stepped forward and spoke.

"Who are you?"

"My name is Ioannes," Jonah replied, giving the Assyrian version of his name.

"You are to come with us. The governor will not allow this disturbance to continue in his beautiful city."

"Will I be taken before the governor?" Jonah asked.

"Not likely," the soldier said with a laugh.

Jonah began to refuse, but strong hands from behind seized him, and he was taken forcefully off the stand. The soldiers marched him away from the crowd and into a maze of streets. He was uncertain of the direction, for the sun had set behind the city wall and the streets twisted and wove into others. One soldier led the way with a lighted torch. They took Jonah to a large, dark building.

Jonah was marched up fifteen steps, across a pillared porch, and through a large wooden door. The room inside was dimly lit by torches, but Jonah could see that it was a large, vaulted hall with arches and passages leading away on all sides. At one of the passages to the right, the soldiers turned. The bare stone walls were lined with crude wooden doors. The guards led Jonah past several doors, then opened one and urged him through it. A man approached, opened the door, and pushed Jonah into a small, smelly cell. The door slammed shut behind him, and the noise echoed down the hall on the other side. Then Jonah heard their retreating footsteps.

For a moment, as he stood in the dark, Jonah was reminded of the three days in the belly of the fish. As in the fish, the darkness was complete—not even a glimmer of torchlight from beneath the door—but as his eyes began to adjust he realized there was a slit of a window high in the wall. Because it was night no light came in except the faint glow of stars.

"O Lord God," Jonah prayed after dropping to his knees, adjusting the covering on his head, and gazing up at the window. "As thou heardest my prayer from the belly of the fish, hear me now in this new prison. It was only through thy power and grace that I was freed from the fish, and I acknowledge that it will only be through thy power and grace that I am able to emerge from this prison to continue the mission thou hast sent me to do."

When he finished, he found a blanket on the floor, wrapped it around himself, and lay on the cold stones. He thought back, trying to remember the last time he had slept comfortably in a room on a sleeping mat. Damascus. He had been given one at the palace of Damascus. And before that? It was Dor. There had been so many nights between Gath-hepher and Nineveh, and most of them were spent on uncomfortable surfaces. However, the prison floor, with a cold that permeated to the core, was worse than the soft, warm desert sand. But not worse than the belly of the fish, Jonah amended. Finally, he slept.

A human face the creature wore,
And hoofs behind and hoofs before,
And flanks with dark runes fretted o'er.
'Twas bull, 'twas mitred Minotaur,
A dead disbowelled mystery:
The mummy of a buried faith
Stark from the charnel without scathe,
Its wings stood for the light to bathe,—
Such fossil cerements as might swathe
The very corpse of Nineveh.

Dante Gabriel Rossetti, "The Burden of Nineveh"

Chapter Fifteen

~~~~~~~~~~~~~~~~~~~~~~~~~~~~~~~~~~

*J*onah was awakened by the opening of the heavy cell door. It swung on its rusted iron hinges, creating a noise that permeated Jonah's dream and brought him abruptly awake. He opened his eyes to see a torch enter the room; its bright light caused him to put up his arm to shade his eyes.

"Get up," a voice barked.

In the light of the torch the man carried, Jonah recognized the now-familiar uniform of an Assyrian soldier, with its conical helmet.

"The gods must be with you, for the governor has determined to see you."

Jonah rose from the floor. He was about to ask for a drink of water when another man entered the cell. This man was dressed in dirty rags, and he ducked when he passed the soldier. He walked with an awkward, shuffling step, carrying a pitcher of water, a small loaf of bread, and a handful of dates. Jonah noticed that the man's left foot was twisted inward. After setting the food on the floor, the second man scurried out like a rodent seeking his hole.

"I will return shortly," the guard informed Jonah, closing the door with another grating protest by the hinges. High in the wall of the cell, a grayish light filtered through the tiny window. Jonah recited the morning prayer while washing his hands—first one, then the other, repeating this three times. The familiar ritual brought comfort to him and helped settle his heart. He knew the words of the soldier reflected the hand of God. He would be taken before the governor, and there he could complete his mission.

When the soldier returned, Jonah had nearly finished his meal. He was led out the way he had entered the night before, and within minutes he found himself riding in a cart toward the palace of the governor, Ninurta-mukin-ahi.

As they neared the palace, Jonah saw that it towered above the other buildings. Terraces and gardens climbed up its heights. They approached it up a long drive, passing fountains and pools, groves, gardens of flowering bushes, and date trees. The scents were more overpowering than the courtyard in Damascus and the expanse was far greater. When the cart stopped at the marble edifice, Jonah was led up many steps and past a pair of colossi—huge statues of gods with the bodies of bulls, the wings of eagles, and the heads of men. He and his escort traveled down marble-tiled hallways lined with carvings in alabaster. One hall led to a central rotunda with carved pillars that reached to the vaulted ceiling far overhead.

Jonah stopped short. The rotunda was so high that he could barely make out the images carved on the supporting pillars. And around the hall were more massive pagan gods, bulls, lions, and other beasts with great expanses of wings and the heads of kings. They stood as sentinels at the pillars and the doorways. A guard pushed Jonah toward one of the intricately carved wooden doors that appeared to be at least the height of five men. Guards in full armor and with large, round shields and straight spears stood on either side of the doors, dwarfed by two colossi standing to either side but staring straight ahead. In the shadow of these silent, pagan gods of Nineveh, Jonah and his escort waited.

Jonah looked about him at the carved pictures on the walls. The craftsmanship, obviously done by skilled artisans, was impressive, but the carvings were of barbarism and cruelty. These carvings represented a culture of bloodthirsty though triumphant warfare. It was a culture that prided itself on the might of its army, the wealth of its acquisitions, and the power of its king. Such a culture centered on the achievements of men. There was no glorifying the one true God.

A creak came as a massive iron bar was lifted from the other side of the double wooden doors. Then, one of the doors swung inward. With a shove, Jonah was flung forward into the court of the governor.

Jonah had heard that governors of Nineveh were powerful men who ruled the province like kings. They sent out decrees, collected tributes, and waged wars. Ninurta-mukin-ahi probably indulged his power as much as any.

Jonah didn't notice the people of the court or try to count the soldiers standing around the perimeter. He looked straight toward to the end of the hall, where Ninurta-mukin-ahi sat on his ornately carved gold throne. He was dressed in deep purple and gold, with pearls woven into the embroidered trim of his hem. He wore a leopard-skin robe and a tall, cylindrical crown, also of gold. In his hand was a long sword, unsheathed but lying across his lap.

Vaguely, Jonah registered that to his left stood various priests in dark robes, some behind carved ebony masks depicting animals. To the right of the governor stood an elderly man with a white beard and a familiar yellow robe over a pale purple tunic. Unknown to Jonah, this man was a beloved uncle of Ninurta-mukin-ahi. The elderly man in yellow bent toward the governor and then motioned to Jonah. The man's words were soft and obviously meant only for the man on the throne.

The governor's vizier, in a long gray robe richly embroidered and studded with jewels, stepped forward and spoke loudly. "Ninurta-mukin-ahi, governor of the vast province of Nineveh, cousin of the king of Assyria, the most powerful of warriors, conqueror of cities, and he who has no rival among the princes of the four quarters of the earth, save only the king, sits in judgment."

Then the chief guard stepped forward and also spoke loudly. "We have brought a man before thee who has prophesied evil concerning thy people. He saith that his god will destroy this great city of Nineveh." The guard's voice echoed in the hall and there was a collective gasp among the spectators. He continued amid indignant whispers. "He saith that unless the people of this city repent of their wickedness, their pride, and the worship of our gods, his Lord God will destroy us in forty days."

Now a brief wave of scornful laughter filled the hall. Then one of the priests beside the governor stepped forward and, with a flourish of his hands, spoke, "Great and wise king, I ask, who is this man that he should stand in judgment against us? Who is his god that he should call our gods false? What god is able to destroy this city, which is protected by the great Ishtar? Behold, who is this man that he should threaten the mighty Ninurta-mukin-ahi? Do not give your attention to this man, O great governor. He is nothing."

Ninurta-mukin-ahi raised his hand, and the priest stepped back. "I am Ninurta-mukin-ahi. Should I be troubled with a fly at the hearth? I have servants to swat such an irritant."

He waved his hand, and two guards took Jonah by the arms to drag him away. Jonah was about to call out, but a spirit of discretion bound his tongue. The guards dragged Jonah from the hall and back through the rotunda. As he was being led back down an adjacent hall, a young boy in a clean, white robe approached the largest guard, greeted him, then showed him a slab of stone with cuneiform carved upon it.

"We wait," the guard said, handing the slab back to the boy.

A single set of footsteps echoed in the distance, coming nearer down an adjoining passage. Then the older man in the yellow robe stepped into the shaft of light coming into the hall from one of the narrow openings high up in the wall.

The guard went closer and bowed deeply. The men shared a muffled conversation, and then the guard returned.

"You will live for now," was all he said, and Jonah was again led away.

For two weeks Jonah fretted in the dark, dirty cell. Two weeks of darkness, bad water, rotted food, and a cold floor, and all the time Nineveh was approaching its day of judgment. There was one moment of hope, but Jonah didn't credit it much since the whole city was about to be destroyed and even one repentant man would suffer with the rest of the population.

It was time for the evening meal when Jonah had been in prison for six days. He was beginning to reconcile himself to spending the rest of his days there, forgotten. The door opened as usual and the now-familiar guard who never spoke stood idly while the man with the twisted foot brought the small portion of food into the room and set it down.

But before the man left, he glanced toward the door. The guard had moved away, and Jonah heard the guard speaking to another not far down the hall. Furtively the man whispered, "Is it true? Is our city going to be destroyed?"

Jonah bent to peer directly into the man's eyes. "Yes, the people of Nineveh will be destroyed as the Lord has spoken because of their wickedness." Jonah reached out to touch the man's arm. "But an individual who faces eternal damnation because of his individual sin may repent. If he were to turn to the Lord God and forsake his sins, his soul could be saved."

The man stood so still that he seemed to turn to stone as he stared at the wall in front of him. Then he asked, "What does one do to forsake their sins and turn to the Lord?"

Jonah could still hear the guards speaking to each other, so he answered the man's question. "He must pray to the Lord, honor his parents, observe the Sabbath day, not commit murder, not steal, not commit adultery."

"I can do these," the man said. "I would like to believe in the Lord God."

Jonah felt a power course through his own body. He stood up straight and looked at the man, then stretched out his hand and laid it on the man's head. "The Lord has forgiven your sins because of your faith. And that you may know the truthfulness of my words, by the power I hold, I command your foot to be healed."

There was a sudden commotion at the door. Two guards rushed in, one holding a torch. "What are you up to?" the other soldier shouted. He swung and knocked the ragged man across the room, then aimed a kick at Jonah's food dish and sent the contents spraying across the wall.

But the man who had been knocked down stood up and exclaimed, "My foot is healed! Blessed be the Lord God and his prophet!"

Everyone turned to look at the man, who held up his newly straight foot, then walked around the room. Then he went to the door and the second guard moved aside for him to exit.

The first guard looked toward Jonah with a frightened face. Then he too left the room, closing the door behind him, but within five minutes a new dish of food was brought. And from that day, the quality of Jonah's meals improved significantly.

The day came when, with his breakfast, he was brought a large basin of water and told to wash himself. "Today, you appear before the governor," the guard informed him.

After much the same procedure as before, Jonah found himself again standing at the end of the vast hall with his eyes fixed on the floor before the governor's throne. Ninurta-mukin-ahi nodded to his vizier, who stepped forward and said, "You may come forward and speak to the governor."

After Jonah walked forward twenty paces, the vizier held up his hand. Jonah stopped and then spoke in a strong, clear voice: "Governor Ninurta-mukin-ahi, I thank you for allowing me to speak. I have traveled far to declare my message. I have walked through your vast city a whole day's journey. I have crossed the desert from Damascus in caravans. And I have traveled the Great Sea in the belly of a fish."

A gasp rose in the hall but was immediately silenced by a stern look from the vizier. "I am sent by Jehovah, the Lord God," Jonah continued, "to declare to this people that unless they repent of their wickedness and pride, they will be destroyed in forty days!"

The vizier, his eyes flashing, sharply replied, "You address Ninurta-mukin-ahi and yet you dare to speak such bold words!"

"They are not my words. I speak the words of the Lord

God, whose Spirit is within me and whose message I deliver. "O wise Ninurta-mukin-ahi, count the days. I first delivered my message many days ago. There now remain but twenty-five days for this vast city to repent!"

Ninurta-mukin-ahi looked at the disheveled old man before him. "I have heard tales of your coming forth from the sea. There has arrived by caravan one who saw a man come from the mouth of a great fish in Sidon. The people of his city say he is a god. Are you this god?"

Jonah saw it was the will of God that his story had come before the governor, that His prophet might receive a second audience. Jonah had not known that Kemuel had sold his new slave, but somehow the man had also made his way to Nineveh. Still, Jonah could not pretend to be what he was not, so he truthfully delivered the message he was commanded to speak.

"I am but the servant and messenger of my God, who prepared the fish to carry me to Sidon."

"It is also said that you are an Israelite. Is your god the god of Israel?"

"Yea, and of all nations." Jonah swallowed as he realized this truth for himself. "He is even the great Jehovah, Creator of heaven and all that is in the heavens—the sun, the moon, and the stars. He is the Creator of earth and all that is on the earth—the mountains, the rivers, the land, and the great seas." Then he added softly, "And all that is in the seas."

The governor leaned forward and rested an elbow on his knee. "If this is so, he is mightier than Ishtar, the great warrior goddess. He is the creator of Ishtar. He is the creator of Nannar, the father of Ishtar. Is this so?"

Jonah took a deep breath and said, "There is no God but the One God. He is the Almighty, the Beginning and the End. His judgments are fair, and his vengeance is mighty."

Ninurta-mukin-ahi sat up straight and motioned toward a guard that stood behind his throne. There was a brief disturbance behind a draped wall, and then a man walked forward. It was a moment before Jonah recognized the man whose foot he had healed in his cell.

The governor looked toward the man and asked, "Is this the man that you claim healed your foot?"

The man's answer was little more than an affirmative squeak. Then Ninurta-mukin-ahi turned toward Jonah. "The guards and his neighbors also testify that he has been lame since birth and that now his foot is healed. What magic is this?"

"It is not magic or trickery. It is the power of the Lord God. This man desired to know more and to believe in the Lord. The Lord knew his heart and forgave his sins. Then, as a sign that this was so, I was able to heal this man's foot."

"Can you heal others?" the governor asked.

Jonah sighed. This was not why he had come to Nineveh. "Which is greater? That this man's foot is healed or that his sins are forgiven and his soul is saved?"

Ninurta-mukin-ahi sat still for a while. Then he looked down at Jonah and asked, "Who are you that your god has sent you to us?"

Jonah repressed a smile of self-deprecation. He represented Jehovah, and despite his own weaknesses, he was the emissary of God. "I am Jonah, the Lord's prophet. I was a disciple of the great prophets Elijah and Elisha. When I was a boy, Elijah raised me from the dead."

Suddenly, Ninurta-mukin-ahi began to wave his hand. "I have heard of this Elijah!" he said triumphantly. "The story came of how he did battle with the priests of Baal and defeated them. Do you know this story?"

Jonah nodded and began to tell the story with the same enthusiasm he had employed in storytelling throughout his journey. He was careful that the truth of the events rang clear.

"Then the fire of the Lord fell, and consumed the burnt sacrifice, and the wood, and the stones, and the dust, and licked up the water that was in the trench. And when all the people saw it, they fell on their faces: and they said, The Lord, he is the God; the Lord, he is the God. And Elijah said unto the people, Take the prophets of Baal; let not one of them escape. And they took them: and Elijah brought them down to the brook Kishon, and slew them there." Jonah finished the story and waited.

Then Ninurta-mukin-ahi looked hard at Jonah and said, "These are powerful words." Then he paused and turned to the man in the yellow robe beside him. The man nodded and the governor continued. "I will think on them." He waved his hand, and guards stepped forward to again escort Jonah back to his cell.

The Lord is . . . longsuffering to us-ward, not willing that any should perish, but that all should come to repentance.

2 Peter 3:9

Chapter Sixteen

෬ඁ෬ඁ෬ඁ෬ඁ෬ඁ෬ඁ෬ඁ෬ඁ෬

The next day, shortly after his morning meal, Jonah was again led to the palace. This time he was taken down different halls and led to a room that was large but smaller than the great hall. Walls of white marble were carved in relief, and the marble floor was inlaid with gold ribbons and brilliant gems. At the end of the hall, on a dais, the governor lounged on a bed of silk cushions. He was eating his morning meal and was attended by three maids in silk veils and cloths that draped their bodies in yellows, greens, and blues. Guards in full uniform, complete with swords, spears, and shields, stood silently to either side. There was no vizier lending formality to the casualness of the audience. But the elderly man who had previously worn a pale yellow robe was seated in a chair to the side of the governor, this time in a robe of sea green with gold trim at the sleeves and hem.

Ninurta-mukin-ahi, dressed in rich purple, lifted his hand, and the man in the chair said loudly, "You may approach."

Jonah went forward to the base of the steps that led up to the dais. He bent to one knee and spoke, "What is your will, Ninurta-mukin-ahi?"

"I have thought on your words. My uncle" —his hand indicated the man in the green robe— "has spoken much concerning them also. They have disturbed our minds with their threats of destruction, and yet strangely, our hearts felt comfort when you spoke."

"What you felt, great governor, is the Spirit of the Lord God, telling your heart that what I spoke is true," Jonah testified.

Ninurta-mukin-ahi did not answer. He sat still and watched the rays of the sun streaming in from a high window. Jonah waited. The trusted uncle waited. The sun moved past the window.

Still, the governor sat in silence. He bowed his head and closed his eyes. Jonah's words had been brief, but he knew that the Spirit of God was working on the governor's heart. At last, he looked about him as though surprised to see that Jonah was still there. Two hours had passed.

Then Ninurta-mukin-ahi, governor of Nineveh, rose from his throne. He crossed to a door, his servants scrambling to arrive before him and open it.

His uncle also arose, turned to Jonah, and said simply, "You may come."

Jonah followed discreetly behind the uncle, who followed the governor. Servants and guards fell in behind them. They passed through passages and gardens. On every side were carved wall murals and the now-familiar colossi. Marble fountains decorated the courtyards, and exotic flowers with strong fragrances filled the air. Then the train of people following the governor entered another door that led to the large hall where Jonah had received his first audiences with

Ninurta-mukin-ahi. The room was filled with the colors of robes and the smell of rich perfumes. People quickly moved aside and took positions along the walls, eager to hear what the governor had to say. A harried vizier was just entering, wiping his mouth on his sleeve, when the governor indicated that he would speak.

"This man has come a great distance into the land of his enemies to bring us a message. He came alone at risk to himself because the God of Israel" —he paused and looked toward Jonah— "and of all nations, spoke to him. When this man spoke the words of the Lord God, he spoke the truth. The Spirit of the Lord has confirmed them to me. And now I know for myself that the Lord God reigns over all the earth. What this prophet spoke is true. We are a prideful and bloodthirsty people. God's vengeance is just. If we are not to be destroyed, we must repent! Therefore, this day I will humble myself before the Lord God, who created the heaven and the earth."

Jonah silently left by the side door through which he had entered. His mission to Nineveh was complete.

Ninurta-mukin-ahi removed his robe and laid it before him. He called for ashes and the cloth that was used to make sacks. The cloth was dark and made from the hair of goats or camels. The governor turned it so that the scratchy hair was toward his skin.

After he was dressed in sackcloth, the governor ordered a servant to pile ashes on the floor. Then Ninurta-mukin-ahi sat in the midst of the ashes, scooped some up with his hand, and sprinkled them over his head. "My joy is perished," he said. Then he raised his head and called for a scribe to record the words that he would speak.

"For three days" —his voice rang out, filling the hall— "let neither man nor beast, herd nor flock, taste anything. Let them not feed, nor drink water, but let man and beast be covered with sackcloth and cry mightily unto the Lord God. Yea, let them turn every one from his evil way, and from the violence that is in their hands!"

He looked to his uncle, who had joined him in mourning. "If we will repent and turn unto God," the governor began, "who can tell but that he will turn away from us his fierce anger?"

The voice of Ninurta-mukin-ahi pierced the people to their hearts. As his beloved uncle joined him in sackcloth among the ashes, soon others did also, and together they prayed mightily unto the Lord God, Creator of heaven and earth.

The words of the governor were written and delivered throughout the city and province of Nineveh all that day, soon spreading to every person in Nineveh and entering the hearts of the people. They recognized their evil ways, humbled themselves, and set about to do as the governor had commanded.

And now, as I said unto you, that because ye were compelled to be humble ye were blessed, do ye not suppose that they are more blessed who truly humble themselves because of the word?

Alma 32:14

Chapter Seventeen

❧❧❧❧❧❧❧❧❧❧❧❧❧❧

Jonah left the palace unchallenged. He exited through a large, open gate and began walking through the streets of Nineveh. He felt hungry and he realized he still had the purse Darius had given him and the few remaining coins from the last caravan master. Jonah followed the sound of a crowd and found his way to a bazaar. He welcomed the warmth of the rising sun after the cold prison where he had spent many nights. He purchased some fried bread, some dates, and a chunk of fresh cheese. Then he wandered until he found a fountain that was not crowded. After drinking deeply from the cool water, he sat down against the warm stones to eat.

Soon something rough and wet wiped across his face. Jonah sat up abruptly and found himself looking into the heavily lashed eyes of a camel. The camel snorted and backed away. As Jonah wiped his face with his sleeve and struggled to stand up, a child laughed. Jonah turned to see a girl with thick braids and large brown eyes.

"The camel doesn't like the way you taste," she said with a grin.

"I don't like the way he smells," Jonah answered.

The little girl giggled.

Jonah smiled at her. "Do you know the way out of the city?"

The girl bit her lip and looked at him. Then she shook her head, picked up the camel's lead rope, and giggled again as she led the camel away.

Jonah considered what he would do next. He had done as God had told him. He had gone to the great and terrible city of Nineveh, seen the people's wickedness and pride, and delivered his message. Now he wanted to leave before the wrath of God came upon the place, but as he looked around the square where the fountain was, he realized he was lost. The sun had begun to cross the sky while he napped, though, and he knew which way was west to the river. Jonah decided he would walk northward until he came to a major road leading to one of the city's gates.

At first he had to pick his way through narrow, twisted streets that wove between the tall houses that clustered around the palace where he had first delivered his message. Sometimes he came upon squares with fountains or long stone canals. He passed a couple of areas where bazaars normally sat, with purveyors actively selling the evening's meals. But everywhere there was a strange urgency of motion. People were not walking idly, and the bazaars were nearly empty. Everyone seemed to be hurrying about.

After a turn in the road, Jonah found himself facing a temple of dark gray stones. Outside the temple was a pool where the priests bathed daily. The pool was empty, and the doors of the temple were closed. Jonah headed down another street, still heading north. He saw mothers gathering children into their arms and rushing them home. He began to wonder if they were fleeing from him.

As Jonah continued to walk, the city streets straightened out and the houses became sparser. He passed orchards with under-ripe fruit, and rich pastures where fat animals grazed. Then he witnessed a new, strange behavior. He watched a man, dressed in sackcloth, enter a pasture of tall grasses carrying an armful of sackcloth. A lad, whose arms were also full, followed him. In the pasture grazed five horses and a dozen goats. The man approached the horses, separated the pieces of sackcloth, and placed one over the head of each animal. The horses were fairly docile, though they snorted as the goatskin was placed on their backs. The man stroked their necks and spoke softly to them while the boy reached under their bellies to tie the skin on. On the other hand, when the goats were approached with the sackcloth, they bucked and ran away. One by one the man and the boy would run after them and try to corner them.

Chuckling to himself, Jonah watched until the man paused to catch his breath, not far from the wall that separated his pasture from the road where Jonah stood.

"Sir," Jonah called, "what are you doing to your animals?"

"Have you not heard?" the man asked. "God will destroy this city unless we repent. He has sent his prophet to tell us so. The king declares that not only we but also our animals are to join in a fast, wearing sackcloth and saying prayers of repentance."

Smote by the man's words, Jonah could not form a reply. The man shrugged and then left in pursuit of his animals.

Jonah leaned against a tall tree along the lane. Casting his eyes upward through the branches toward the heavens, he cried out, "O Lord, was not this my concern when I was at

Jerusalem? Did I not say to my friend and thy faithful servant
Aziel that I feared that Nineveh would repent? Who is mightier
than Assyria? If they repent, can they not be the instrument
in thy hands to destroy my people? Therefore I fled before
thee, for I knew that thou art a gracious God, and merciful,
slow to anger, and of great kindness, and would turn aside thy
judgment."

Jonah dropped his head and asked himself what he had
done. Would this lead to the destruction of his own people?
"Therefore now, O Lord," he prayed in a choked voice, "take,
I beseech thee, my life from me." Jonah sobbed and sank to
the earth, hiding his face in his hands. "For it is better for me
to die than to live."

A voice, firm but kind, came to him: "Doest thou well to be
angry? Have you forgotten so soon that I am the Lord God?
Was your life not in my hands when I brought you here?"

Emotionally drained, Jonah arose and walked toward a
distant gate that rose above a city wall to the east. He would
leave the city as quickly as possible. He had always believed
that God was just, and certainly the people of Nineveh were
more wicked and depraved than any people on earth. Surely a
bit of sackcloth and three days of prayers would not change the
decrees of the great Jehovah, who had said He would destroy
Nineveh.

Jonah angrily recalled all the things he had seen in Nineveh.
He remembered the unchaste women and the unchaste men
who purchased their favors. He remembered the proud people
with their fine clothes and jewels, and the poor who were
treated badly by the rich. He recalled the evil priests and their
dark practices. He remembered the smell of the slave market
and the ridicule of the people when he stood to preach. The
more he thought on the pride of Nineveh, the more he became

sure that such a city could not repent.

When he arrived at the eastern gate, he glanced back at the wicked city. "Twenty-five days," he said as he passed through the gate. He thought to himself, *It will be a few weeks yet before the caravans begin to travel again across the desert. I will have time to witness the destruction of Nineveh.*

Then Jonah climbed the gentle slopes of the foothills behind Nineveh. It was dark when he curled up in his robe beside a clear stream and fell asleep.

After several days of wandering the foothills and working for farmers to obtain food, Jonah decided it was time to establish a place of his own. He purchased tools with some money from the bag Darius had given him, which was nearly depleted, then spent two days building a booth that was long enough for him to stretch out and sleep in. The structure had three walls, and the top was only partially covered with boughs so that at night Jonah could see the stars.

When his booth was complete, with the open side to the west with a view of the city, Jonah sat inside like a spectator preparing to watch a battle. The prophetic deadline would arrive in just a few days.

It was height of the hot, dry season, and the booth offered limited relief from the heat of the sun. After midday when the sun began to lower in the western sky, the most intense heat of the day poured directly into the booth. By the second afternoon, Jonah felt uncomfortable and resentful, frustrated with his own lack of planning. He was convinced that the people of Nineveh were too deeply wrapped in their wickedness to truly repent. He had no means of leaving the city, and staying to observe its destruction was proving to be a trial. Had the Lord forgotten his prophet now that Jonah had delivered the divine message?

Tired, discouraged, and hot, Jonah did not notice that the

gourd growing beside his booth had begun to flourish. Nourished by a stream, it grew until it covered the booth where Jonah sat. Climbing up the eastern wall, it spread its broad leaves over the top of the booth, twining among the boughs and hanging down the front, shading the interior from the western sun. It grew rapidly, and by the third day, sitting inside his now-shaded booth, Jonah recognized it as a gift from the Lord.

In the coolness provided by the gourd, Jonah felt lighthearted and happy. He felt the love of God as he sat there, and he knew he had been fully forgiven for his disobedience in fleeing to Tarshish. He had done as God had asked, and his heart was comforted. For one night he slept peacefully, delivered from his grief. The next day was day forty, as he calculated it. He settled down to sleep, contemplating the means God might use to destroy Nineveh. Would it be fire rained down from heaven, or a great earthquake, or a large army—perhaps the Babylonians—from the south? Jonah tucked his worn robe around him and slept peacefully, convinced that whatever means God employed to destroy the city, he would protect his prophet.

But during the night the larvae from a worm that had been wrapped in the leaves of the gourd began to feast. By morning the plant was withered, becoming brittle even as the horizon began to glow with the early morning light.

Jonah noticed the withering vine as the sun mounted in the sky, and he plucked the worst of the dying leaves to relieve the plant. "Do not forsake me," he exclaimed as he dug around the gourd's roots so that the water might penetrate the ground.

The vine, however, continued to shrivel. Jonah increased the flow of the stream to the roots. Soon the ground was a pool of water at the base of the vine, yet it continued to decay. By noon that day, the vine was brown and the gourd was shriveled.

When Jonah inspected the leaves, he found the larvae that had caused the damage. Grabbing a handful of infested leaves, he threw them away in anger. "Why do you think to destroy this gourd?"

The sun was now high in the sky, and a wind began to gather to the east where the hills pulled back to the north, leaving the expanse of a plain where Nineveh was built. The wind grew, blowing away the dry leaves on the vine. Jonah wrapped his robe closer around himself as the wind continued to grow. The vine snapped, and the shriveled gourd fell to the ground. Finally, when all trace of the protecting vine was gone, the wind ceased and the sun beat down upon Jonah. Weak from his labor and frustrated that he had been unable to save the vine, he fell to the earth. Then Jonah recalled what day it was. He stood up immediately and looked down at the vast city that stretched for miles to his left and to his right. Nineveh remained undisturbed. The sun glinted off the towers of its great palaces, temples, and shrines.

Jonah strained to see if there was dust from an approaching army or clouds from an approaching storm coming toward this vast, wicked city. There was nothing, only the sun moving downward toward evening and the close of the day. It would end as a regular day and not as the momentous one he had traveled so far to prophesy of.

The sun angled to where Jonah stood, as if aiming its full afternoon strength on him. He began to sweat. Then he thought again of the gourd. Standing where he was, trying to shade his eyes and see the city below, he began to call upon God in frustration. "Why dost thou spare the people of Nineveh?" he cried. "Surely they have committed great abominations against thee, and yet thou allowest a small worm to destroy such a fine vine that has committed no sin but has given shade to my poor head!" Jonah kicked at the dirt in his booth.

Then the Lord spoke again to Jonah's heart. "Thou hast had pity on the gourd, for which thou has not labored to plant, neither did you make it grow; which plant came up in a night, and perished in a night. Yet thou carest not for Nineveh. I created all things. I created the gourd to give you shade. And I created the inhabitants of Nineveh. Should I not desire to spare my children? Did I not bring you here that they might repent? And now that they have humbled themselves in sackcloth and cried to me with repentant hearts, should I not spare Nineveh? And remember the six score thousand children who cannot discern between right and wrong, or even their right hand from their left? Are they to be destroyed? And even all the dumb cattle of the fields? Do you pity a gourd more than those?"

A slight breeze arose and a cloud covered the sun, giving Jonah a moment of relief. And then God gave his final message, the one Jonah had missed, though he had been the messenger who had delivered it to Nineveh.

With a voice that penetrated Jonah even as that first morning in Jerusalem, the Lord declared: "I am the Lord God; all men are mine. I will give to all nations my love and to all that repent my forgiveness. I am a God of justice and of mercy! Through my only begotten Son who will come into the world, all mankind can feel of my mercy. Can thou not forgive them also?"

The winds were still, and the sun began to set. One by one the stars pierced the growing darkness to fill the sky with their brilliance. And Jonah reconsidered.

Memories began to come back to him. First he recalled when, as a boy, he had awakened in Elijah's room after being raised from the dead by the prophet. Had he done anything to deserve the gift of life a second time? When Elijah and Jonah's mother had told Jonah of the events of that day, they had said it was God's mercy that he was alive.

Jonah thought of when the armies of the Syrians had surrounded the hilltop town of Dothan. Wasn't it an act of mercy that God had sent his unseen hosts that gathered on the hillside as an army of fire? Then the Lord compounded that mercy by causing the Syrian army to be blinded at Elisha's request. Now Jonah understood that Elisha could have called upon the heavenly army to slay the Syrians in an act of justice. But Elisha had shown mercy toward them by having them struck blind instead, that he might lead them away to a situation where they would accept their defeat and peacefully return home.

Then Jonah recalled when he had been cast into the sea by the sailors. Although he could swim—not as well, it was true, now that he was an old man—no man could swim in waves that large. Though he hadn't realized it at the time, being swallowed by the fish had actually saved his life. Then the Lord had caused the fish to carry Jonah to a port and vomit him out on the sand unharmed, so that he could begin his journey again. Most mercifully, the Lord had forgiven him for running to Tarshish and then, without reserve or condition, had given him a second chance.

Jonah paused to wonder how many times in his life he had received the mercy of the Lord. How many times had he been given a second chance? His very journey into Assyria was one of providential protection. Had he justly earned such blessings?

Suddenly, Jonah realized that even the loss of the gourd had been an act of mercy that had shown him the Lord's boundless love for all His people. Jonah connected the blindness imposed on the Syrians, the great fish that swallowed him, and the dying of the gourd. He realized that though they may seem severe and punishing when they happen, some difficult events are actually acts of mercy.

Jonah recognized that though the Lord God was just, He was also merciful. The concept had come slowly to Jonah. Justice gave men confidence that there would be natural consequences for their choices. When kept, the laws of God brought blessings; when broken, they brought misery. It was not a random universe with unpredictable outcomes. However, mercy meant that repentant mistakes could be forgiven—that when people humbled themselves and repented, hearts were changed, and the Lord's mercy offered a second chance. Jonah had taught it to the man in prison and to the governor of Nineveh, but he had not really believed it himself until now.

In the deep hours of the night, Jonah pondered this truth. He began to understand something else as well. He had thought that perhaps he had been the best choice to come to Nineveh, or at least the best the Lord could find. Perhaps it was his language skills, his learning, or his faithfulness—until now he had not thought about the reason. But now he knew that his call to Nineveh was also an act of mercy to him. Because of his experience, he had finally come to understand the Lord's kindness, love, and mercy. Jonah accepted that the people of Nineveh had been forgiven, and so had he.

The next day, Jonah rose early, descended the foothills, and walked through a gate into Nineveh. The city seemed more peaceful and calm—a completely different feeling than he had experienced there just forty-one days previously. He met a stooped peasant woman carrying water in a jar.

"Excuse me, mother," he said, "do you know the meaning of this day?"

"Yes," she answered, her face lighting up. "This is the day

after the Lord God spared our city. Today we still live."

Jonah smiled. "Let me carry your load, and perhaps I may serve you until I find work to take me home."

"Home?"

"Yes, I come from far away." Jonah thought of the long journey ahead. "It is time for me to return."

Sources and Historical Notes

While writing *The Terrible City*, I encountered questions such as "Where is Tarshish?" and "How did Jonah get to Nineveh?" These questions led me to find all the information I could about events that occurred more than 2700 years ago, as well as the places where they happened and the lifestyles of the people involved. Finding answers was often like participating in an archaeological dig, where mere shards of pottery or other pieces and remnants of the past became vital clues to the story. It was thrilling to stumble onto a new source or bit of information that would contribute to the solidity of a story that much of the world today considers merely a tall tale. (In fact, many biblical scholars place Jonah's story, along with the stories of Noah and Daniel, in the genre of children's literature.) What I found was that there was more to Jonah than a "big fish story."

Some of the most startling details came from ancient or Rabbinic traditions that are firmly taught today as essential history, such as the idea that Jonah was the son of the woman of Zarephath (Sarephta) that was raised from the dead by Elijah (see Kark Budde, Emil G. Hirsch, and Soloman Schecter, http://www.jewishencyclopedia.com/view.jsp?artid=388&letter=J,

accessed Sept. 12, 2009). This detail, however, created a dilemma with logistics—particularly Jonah's age. The best estimates place the events between Elijah and the widow of Zarephath between 850 and 860 BC, yet Jonah traveling to Nineveh between 760 and 785 BC. That would make Jonah well over 100 years old when he traveled to Nineveh. Then I found this quote: "He is said to have attained a very advanced age (more than 120 years according to Seder 'Olam; 130 according to Sefer Yuhasin), while Ecclesiastes Rabbah viii. 10 holds that the son (Jonah) of the Zarephath widow never died" (ibid., accessed Sept. 23, 2009). I decided it was not unfeasible; nevertheless, since ancient historical dates are so difficult to be accurate with, I chose to write Jonah as an energetic 70-plus-year-old man when he goes to Nineveh.

Another Rabbinic tradition is that Jonah's wife is "an example of a woman voluntarily assuming duties not incumbent on her." She is also "remembered as having made the pilgrimage to Jerusalem on the 'regel' [holiday]" (http://www.jewishencyclopedia.com/view.jsp?artid=388&letter=J#i xzz0SGwiIKSU, accessed Sept. 2009).

Considering Jonah's miraculous beginnings with Elijah, I was not surprised to learn that it is believed that he received his prophetic appointment from Elisha, and that it was by his command that Jonah anointed Jehu (see http://www.jewishencyclopedia.com/view.jsp?artid=388&letter=J#ixzz0S R5bbGQs, accessed Sept. 2009).

Jonah is also mentioned in 2 Kings 14:25, during the reign of Jeroboam (II): "He restored the coast of Israel from the entering of Hamath unto the sea of the plain, according to the word of the Lord God of Israel, which he spake by the hand of his servant Jonah, the son of Amittai, the prophet, which was of Gath-hepher."

Geographically, locating cities consisted of searching through various sources and maps to bring everything together and give the correct names to cities for that time period. Tarshish became a real puzzle, with conflicting opinions among scholars. The fact is that nobody knows for certain where Tarshish was. "The Septuagint, the Greek version of the Old Testament, translated Tarshish as Carthage. Josephus and others identified Tarshish with Tarsus in Cilicia. Julius Africanus thought it was a name for Rhodes or Cyprus. Eusebius and Hippolytus conjectured that the city of Tartessos in Iberia (southern Spain), mentioned by Herodotus and other ancient writers, was the biblical Tarshish. Modern authors are divided between Tartessos (Iberia) and Tarsus (Cilicia)" (www.varchive.org/nldag/tarshish.htm). Still, the expression "ships of Tarshish" became a general term for ships sailing on long-distance voyages. Many consider the name Tarshish to refer to foreign lands in general. (See ibid.)

> *Where is the wealth of ages that heaped thy princely mart?*
>
> *The pomp of purple trappings; the gems of Syrian art;*
>
> *The silken goats of Kedar, Sabaen's spicy store;*
>
> *The tributes of the islands thy squadrons homeward bore,*
>
> *And evermore the surges chant forth their vain desire:*
>
> *"Where are the ships of Tarshish, the might ships of Tyre?"*
> (Bayard Taylor, *Tyre*)

It was also fascinating to learn the details of the individuality of each city. Zarephath was known as a place of kilns and pottery making. The name Joppa (which is now Jaffa [yä´ fä], the name coming from the Hebrew word *yafo*, meaning "beauty") is traditionally thought to have come from Japheth, the son of Noah, who founded the city of Joppa forty years after the Flood. (The modern city of Tel Aviv was founded on the outskirts of Jaffa in 1909. Today it encompasses the ancient city.) Joppa, one of the oldest cities on earth and an important port, has a shallow, rocky harbor, making it unfit for sailing vessels to enter any closer than a mile from shore.

Sidon, a key Phoenician city, is where the valuable purple dye came from. The small Murex shells, harvested from the sea via nets, were broken apart so that the pigment could be extracted. It was so rare that it became the mark of royalty. Today in Sidon, there is a mound of debris called Murex Hill. This artificial hill (one hundred meters long and fifty meters high) was formed by the accumulation of refuse from the purple dye factories of Phoenician times. Mosaic tiling found at the top of the mound suggests that Roman buildings once stood there. Today houses, buildings, and a cemetery cover the hill. Broken murex shells can still be seen on the lower part of the hill.

Damascus, which vies for the claim "oldest city in the world," was the capital of the Aramaeans during the time of Jonah. (About 50 years later, in 732 BC, Damascus would be captured and destroyed by the Assyrians under Tiglath-Pileser. It would be the end of the reign of the Aramaean kings, and they as well as the Aramaean people would be carried away captive into Assyria, where much of their language would be adopted.) Damascus is situated on a plateau at the edge of the desert along one of the major caravan routes. Like many cities of its day, it was not laid out with a master plan, but had twisting, narrow streets that sometimes had right-angle bends. When the Romans rebuilt and expanded the "old city," the main street from the west gate to the east gate was covered.

Luke refers to it as the "street called straight." Mark Twain wrote of this street in Damascus, "The street called Straight is straighter than a corkscrew, but not as straight as a rainbow. St. Luke is careful not to commit himself; he does not say it is the street which is straight, but 'the street which is called Straight.' It is the only facetious remark in the Bible, I believe" (Mark Twain, *The Innocents Abroad*, 1869).

The name of Tadmor—a city believed to have been built by King Solomon—was changed to Palmyra ("Place of Palms") under the Roman Emperor Tiberius. Today, it is again called Tadmor. Resafa is a city in the desert with no natural source of water from rivers or springs, but the rainfall is sufficient to fill large cisterns that were built there in ancient times. It was also a major fortress under the Assyrian Empire. Unlike other cities of haphazard layouts, Harran, the city at the crossroads of trade routes in the north, was originally designed after the plan of the city of Ur—in the shape of the moon to honor the god Nannar. The streets run parallel to the circumference of the city walls, with other streets running straight toward the center, connecting the circular ones toward the center hill. The name Harran comes from the Sumerian and Akkadian term *Harran-U*, meaning "journey and caravan crossroad."

A few basic geographical names that have changed include the Great Sea, which is today known as the Mediterranean Sea. It was also called the Upper Sea (the Lower Sea being the Red Sea). The Sea of Chinnereth is also known as the Sea of Galilee. However, its names are numerous: Bahr Tubariya, Ginnosar, Lake of Gennesaret, Lake of Gennesar, Sea of Chinneroth, Sea of Kinnereth, Sea of Tiberias, Lake of Tiberias, Waters of Gennesaret, and Yam Kinneret. The rabbis said of Chinnereth, "Although God has created seven seas, yet He has chosen this one as His special delight" (http://www.

bibleplaces.com/seagalilee.htm, accessed Oct. 8, 2009). This lake, as well as the Great Sea, is as historical as Jerusalem in the land of Israel, though even more ancient, playing key roles from the beginning in the development of history.

Other geographical names include the Abana River, which is now known as the Barada River; the Great Desert, which is the Arabian Desert; and the oasis around Damascus, now called the Al Ghuta.

Trade routes were also an elusive detail, but I have tried to represent them as accurately as possible on the map at the beginning of the book. Ships would sail along the coast of the Great Sea, with port cities spaced strategically about one day apart. In that time, much navigation was done by sight of land, although the ship's pilot was considered a chief position and the charts were esteemed of more value than the cargo. The caravan route that followed these port cities on land from one to the next was called the Way of the Sea. These trade routes traveled inland to such major destinations as the city of Nineveh.

Various kingdoms made up Jonah's world—the Phoenicians, the Philistines, the Aramaeans, the kingdom of Judah, and the kingdom of Israel. Each of these relatively small kingdoms lived in the threatening shadow of the great kingdom of Assyria to the north and east. Within each kingdom were major cities such as Sidon, Damascus, Samaria, Jerusalem, and Nineveh. Except for the Hebrew nations, major cities had "patron" gods and temples built to those gods, male and female. The worship in these temples was, at best, drunken, debased, and evil, but also included the barbaric, unfathomable act of citizens sacrificing their own children to idols. The people of this world were very superstitious, and each person often prayed to whichever god fitted his need. As was common, I have given Jonah's ship the carved images of the Cabeiri, which originated from the Greek myth that identifies them as divine craftsmen, sons or grandsons of Hephaestus, who were worshiped as protectors of sailors.

Among the city gods are Nannar, later known as Sin, the god of Harran and Ur. Ishtar/Inanna and her twin, Utu/Shamash, are children of Nannar/Sin. The goddess Ishtar represents the planet Venus. (A continent on Venus is called Ishtar Terra by astronomers today.) Ishtar was celebrated and invoked as the force of life. She was also invoked as a goddess of war, battles, and the chase, particularly among the warlike Assyrians. Before a battle, Ishtar was believed to appear to the Assyrian army, clad in battle array and armed with bow and arrow.

Idol worship penetrated into the kingdoms of Judah and Israel, and it was this concern that occupied much of the efforts of the prophets. It was a destructive stumbling block for Solomon. In the days of Jeroboam, king of Israel, when Israel and Judah were first divided, Jeroboam became jealous of the feast days that caused many of his people to make a pilgrimage to Jerusalem. He had received reports that once there, the people had begun to stay, and he feared he would lose more Israelites to Rehoboam, king of Judah. So Jeroboam had two golden calves made, fashioned after the manner of the calf that Aaron had built. He had them placed in Dan and at Bethel for the people to worship, offering them alternative idols to the pagan gods. Bethel was chosen for its location on the border with Judah; Jeroboam hoped to stop the people on pilgrimage from continuing their journey further.

My research led me to many other fragments that began to combine to create a complete picture of Jonah's world. When I tried to determine who was king of Assyria at the time of Jonah, I came across two articles explaining that Nineveh was a provincial city of Assyria ruled over by a governor. The Hebrew translation calls him the "king of Nineveh"—noticeably *not* the "king of Assyria." (For further explanation, see Paul Ferguson, "Who was the King of Nineveh in Jonah 3:6," http://www.tyndalehouse.com/tynbul/library/TynBull_1996_47_2_05_Ferguson_KingOfNinevehJonah3.DOC, accessed Oct. 2, 2009; and Paul J. N. Lawrence, "Assyrian Nobles and the Book of Jonah," http://www.tyndalehouse.com/tynbul/library/TynBull_1986_37_06_Lawrence_AssyrianNobles_Jonah.pdf, accessed Oct. 2, 2009). Mr. Ferguson further explains that rare artifacts with official names engraved on them reveal that "Governors of Nineveh held office in Nineveh in 789 and 761 BC. Their names were Ninurta-mukin-ahi and Nabu-mukin-ahi, respectively. This would be the general period in which Jonah would have performed his ministry. It is possible, but by no means certain, that either might have been the official described in Jonah 3." I simply chose the name of the first governor to use in the story.

Nineveh, as the destination of Jonah's call, becomes a central focus of the story. In the nineteenth and twentieth centuries, many archaeologists were allowed to explore the site of Nineveh, which is located in today's desert plain across the Tigris River from Mosul in Iraq. Austen Henry Layard, Esq., was among the early explorers. From 1845 to 1854, Layard led archaeological expeditions to excavate Nineveh. I referenced his book, *Nineveh and Its Remains* (London: John Murray, Albermarle Street, 1850), for many of my details. Also used was George Smith's work *Assyrian Discoveries: An Account of Explorations and Discoveries on the Site of Nineveh, During 1873–1874* (New York: Scribner, Armstrong and Co., 1875). This later book is an account of Smith's second expedition to Nineveh in 1873 at the expense of the British Museum. Smith translated several works from the site, including the *Epic of Gilgamesh.*

In the archaeological evidence found by these men and those who followed, a predominate theme was the ruthless, empirical nature of the Assyrians. The Assyrians built palaces and temples in which they recorded in stone their most horrifying tortures and mutilations, each king trying to maim and gore the vanquished more zealously than the last. Nearly 80 years after Jonah's mission, King Sennacherib (704–681 BC) razed 89 towns and 820 villages to the ground, carrying off 208,000 prisoners to be resettled elsewhere. When he defeated Babylon, he burned it to its foundation. Then he killed every soul in the city. He purportedly claimed, "I cut off their heads, and outside their cities, like heaps of grain, I piled them up" (Thomas L. Brodie, *Genesis as Dialogue, A Literary, Historical, and Theological Commentary* [Oxford: Oxford University Press, 2001, 507]).

Although it is Sennacherib that built Nineveh up to its full grandeur, it was still very impressive during Jonah's time. And it wasn't until Sennacherib that the ramparts along the river were built to their full height, and the walls encompassing the city pierced by fifteen massive gates. Nevertheless, I have included one of the gates for Jonah to pass beneath as an illustration of the scale of the city he is about to enter and as representation of what it was like to live beneath the shadow of the Assyrian Empire.

There were two significant questions concerning the story found in the Bible. The first was "What kind of fish swallowed Jonah?" One scholar stated, "The Bible doesn't actually specify what sort of marine animal swallowed Jonah. Most people assume that it was a cachalot (also known as the sperm whale). It may very well have been a white shark. The Hebrew phrase used in the Old Testament, *gadowl dag*, literally means 'great fish.' The Greek used in the New Testament is *këtos*, which simply means 'sea creature.' There are at least two species of Mediterranean marine life that are known to be able to swallow a man whole. These are the cachalot and the white shark. Both creatures are known to prowl the Mediterranean and have been known to Mediterranean sailors since antiquity. Aristotle described both species in his 4th Century BC *Historia Animalium*" (www.gotquestions.org/Jonah-whale.html). It is in the King James version of Matthew that Jonah's fish is called a whale. The Lord refers to Jonah's three days in the belly of the fish as a sign of his death, declaring: "An evil and adulterous generation seeketh after a sign; and there shall no sign be given to it, but the sign of the prophet Jonas: For as Jonas was three days and three nights in the whale's belly; so shall the Son of man be three days and three nights in the heart of the earth" (Matthew 12:39–40). However, in other Bible translations the Lord calls Jonah's captor a "great fish," a "huge fish," even a "sea monster." As one source put it, "Matthew 12:40 says that the creature is a whale, but the original Greek from which it was translated calls it a "sea monster."

To me, it doesn't really matter what type of fish it was, whether whale, shark, or one that God had prepared that is unknown to us today. The miracles are that the fish was there to swallow Jonah rather than let him drown, that Jonah survived in the belly of the creature, and that the fish vomited Jonah upon the shore, where he received his second call to go to Nineveh.

The second scriptural question was, What is this booth Jonah builds at the end of the story? Each fall, Jews celebrate the holiday of the Sukkah as it is explained in Exodus 23:16: "And the Feast of Ingathering at the end of the year, when you gather in the results of your work from the field" (see also Leviticus 23:42–43). During this holiday, it is customary for families to erect a booth where they take all their full meals. Devout Jews even sleep in the booth. The roof is open or only partially covered so that the stars can be seen. It is a reminder to them, at a time of harvest and plenty, when Israel fled from Egypt and lived in the wilderness in tents. Observers of this holiday reflect, "Indeed it is well in wealth to remember your poverty, in distinction your insignificance, in high offices your position as a commoner, in peace your dangers in war, on land the storms on sea, in cities the life of loneliness" (Rabbi David Goinkin, "Seven Reasons for Sukkah Sitting," http://www.myjewishlearning.com/holidays/Jewish_Holidays/Sukkot/At_Home/The_Sukkah/Meaning/Seven_Reasons_for_Sukkah.shtml?HYJH, accessed Oct. 7, 2009). Although in my story the fall season has not yet arrived, I have fashioned Jonah's booth after the model of the booths used during this holiday. It also fits with the gourd that grows up and shades his booth.

After these and many other questions were answered, after hours of fascinating research and discovery, what I found was that in the end, the story of Jonah, with all its colorful historic details and association with some of the Bible's greatest prophets, was still simply a story about the love of God for all of mankind and His everlasting mercy, both to populations as a whole and to individuals.

Susan Dayley is the second of nine children. She has loved stories and the magic of words since childhood, and she spent many nights telling adventure stories to her sisters. Susan would often escape to a grassy meadow or climb a backyard willow tree to read a beloved book. As a youth, her favorites included *Joe's Boys, Call of the Wild,* and *Black Beauty.*

In school, Susan loved best the writing classes, but despite being encouraged to publish her stories, she never took the leap until now. For several years, Susan taught elementary education at private LDS-based schools, where she indulged her love of literature, history, language, and the scriptures.

In addition to writing, Susan enjoys reading classic literature, exploring trails, gardening, BYU football, traveling, and above all, spending time with her husband and their children.